Praise For *The Dahlonega Sisters Series*

"What an absolute pleasure it was to read The Dahlonega Sisters by Diane M How. This moving family drama, laced with mystery, is a beautiful, touching romance and a lot more besides. Diane M How brings to life such wonderful characters that if they were real people, I would love to meet them."

5-star review by Jewel Hart, Editor
Book Marketing Specialist
Author Visibility/Brand Consultant
Chick-Lit Cafe-Bookstagram

"You can't help but like these women and you are going to want to get to know them better. Each has their own unique personality, and the conclusion wraps it all up in one neat package, although I believe there is a follow-on story. I'm looking forward to reading it. This story will keep you happily immersed in the sisters' world for a few hours."

Congratulations on your 5-star review!
—Reviewed By Anne-Marie Reynolds
for *Readers' Favorite*

"I was thoroughly charmed by this story of sisterhood /family, return to faith, small town living, and second chance at love. The main characters (Mutzi, Marge, Rose Ellen, and April) are all relatable and real. Ms. How gave each of them distinct personalities right from the start with quirks and mannerisms that make them likable and sympathetic."

4.5-star review by Maida Malby, *Carpe Diem Chronicles*

The Dahlonega Sisters received 28 out of 30 points and some pleasant comments from Writer's Digest

"Despite the very serious and even heartbreaking problems that each of the characters face, *The Dahlonega Sisters* has a delightful charm to it that draws the reader almost effortlessly into the lives of the McGilvray sisters and the town of Dahlonega. Mutzi is every bit as quirky as her name, and not only is she a character that readers want to root for, her energy and spirit move the story forward.

The curse of the ring is such an intriguing plot point that was well executed. Whether or not the ring is actually cursed doesn't even matter, as the struggles that the sisters and Emily face while holding onto the ring advance the plot, and sometimes even in directions that readers don't anticipate, such as when the prim and proper Marge's car breaks down, and she secretly relishes the tow truck operator's appreciation of her rear end. This moment reveals a side of Marge that readers haven't yet seen, yet appreciate.

Both Mutzi and Marge have layers and dimensionality to their characters and personalities that are slowly and delightfully revealed as the story progresses. That said, I felt that Rose Ellen's character wasn't as clearly defined as her younger sisters. We know by the end of the novel that, despite her financial success, Rose Ellen is lonely and longs for a relationship, but simultaneously distrusts men, I feel that this is more told to the reader, rather than shown. Whereas readers get to see Mutzi's pain and superstition in the way in which she behaves, such as her refusal to go to church because she believes that God is angry with her.

The Dahlonega Sisters, The Gold Miner Ring is an inspiring tale of loss, love, and forgiveness that readers will enjoy falling in love with."

Judge, 28th Annual Writer's Digest
Self-Published Book Awards

The bond Marge, Rose, and Mutzi share is a beautiful one that makes anyone feel grateful for the relationships they share with their loved ones. It sure made me grateful for the one I share with my twin sister, Diza. I sympathized with the character of Chuck and was charmed by the beautiful ending where he finds familyhood and a sense of belonging that he deserved from the very start. This book was an absolute delight to read, and I found myself glued to it all the way through. I really wish there would have been a movie for it because I visualized everything from start to finish and the characters were so relatable and realistic. So comforting, and it truly brings to life the magic of family love. When the Dahlonega Sisters get behind a project, they can move mountains indeed!

Highly recommended! Saania (goodreads)

I just finished the 3rd book in *The Dahlonega Sisters* series and I loved it! Thank you, Diane, for this wonderful story! Well done! Can't wait to see what you give us next!

Kathy Ray

I finished the first Dahlonega Sisters book yesterday and liked it so much, I read all of the second book today!!

Keep writing, Mary Beth Ohlmes

Skipping Stone Lodge

NEW BEGINNINGS

—⁓—

Diane M. How

Silver Lining Publishing, L.L.C.
ST. PETERS, MISSOURI

Published by Silver Lining Publishing, L.L.C.
70 Oakridge West Drive
St. Peters, Missouri 63376 (United States of America)

Publisher's Note: This is a work of fiction. Names, characters, places, and incidents are a product of the author's imagination. Locales and public names are sometimes used for atmospheric purposes. Any resemblance to actual people, living or dead, or to businesses, companies, events, institutions, or locales is completely coincidental. Although some real-life iconic places are depicted in settings, all situations and people related to those places are fictional.

Publisher's Cataloging-in-Publication Data
provided by Five Rainbows Cataloging Services

Names: How, Diane M., author.
Title: Skipping Stone Lodge : new beginnings / Diane M. How.
Description: St. Peters, MO : Silver Lining Publishing, 2024.
Identifiers: LCCN 2024921609 (print) | ISBN 978-1-73403-839-2 (paperback) | ISBN 978-1-73403-838-5 (ebook)
Subjects: LCSH: Ex-convicts--Fiction. | Sisters--Fiction. | Family life--Fiction. | Small cities--Fiction. | Dahlonega (Ga.)--Fiction. | BISAC: FICTION / Family Life / Siblings. | FICTION / Small Town & Rural. | FICTION / Southern.
Classification: LCC PS3608.O89 S55 2024 (print) | LCC PS3608.O8 9 (ebook) | DDC 813/.6--dc23.

Dedicated To

Denise Judd and Rose Ellen Koutsobinas.
A woman is fortunate to have one bestie.
I've been blessed with two.
Love you both to the moon and back.

Dahlonega, Georgia, USA

Nestled in the northern Georgia mountains, the quaint historical gold rush town of Dahlonega (duh lon eh ga) opens its arms to welcome hundreds of thousands of visitors each year. From listening to roaring waterfalls, taking tranquil walks in the foothills of the Blue Ridge Mountains, or shopping until you drop at the delightfully unique shops in the attractive town square, there is a magnetic appeal which satisfies each and every tourist. Many have grown roots after just one stay.

Dahlonega, the location of the first major US Gold Rush, celebrates its history with a gold museum in the center of the town square and two gold mines where visitors may pan for gold and gems. The annual Gold Rush Festival held in October is a must to experience as well as Christmas on Candy Cane Lane hosted by the Dahlonega Woman's Club each December.

The Dahlonega Sisters, Mutzi, Marge, and Rose Ellen are fictional characters...at least to others. To me, they are legendary women who enjoy bouts of sister-fussing, are a force to be reckoned with when problems arise, and have become family to many readers. If you have yet to meet them, while it's not necessary, you might want to begin their journey by reading *The Gold Miner Ring* followed by *Veins of Gold* and *Golden Adventures*. Mystery, romance, and a good dose of humor fill the pages of each novel.

The sisters are embarking on a new adventure in *Skipping Stone Lodge*. If you know them well, welcome home. If this is your first introduction to the sisters, I hope you will find them as endearing as I do.

Cast of Characters

Mutzi McGilvray Parks: Dog lover, laughter-seeking, quirky, and superstitious sister of Marge, Chuck, and Rose Ellen. A triplet to Marge and Chuck.

Marge McGilvray Ledbetter: Level-headed sister of Mutzi, Chuck, and Rose Ellen. President of the Dahlonega Woman's Club. Always dependable. Talks to her late husband, George. A triplet to Mutzi and Chuck.

Rose Ellen McGilvray Preston Montelini: Oldest of the siblings. A little haughty, often an attention seeker, and wife of Roberto. Mother of April. Grandmother of Savannah.

Chuck—aka Milford Charles Hansen: Brother of Mutzi, Marge, and Rose Ellen. Illegally separated from his triplet sisters at birth. Placed in an orphanage at age five.

United with The Dahlonega Sisters on his 65th birthday.

Buddy Jenkins: Homeless young man Chuck invites to work at Skipping Stone Lodge.

April Preston: Daughter of Rose Ellen. Lawyer on extended maternity leave and mother of Savannah.

Paul Stevenson: April's husband. Lawyer.

Savannah Stevenson: Infant daughter of April and Paul.

Roberto Montelini: Rose Ellen's husband. Curator at the Georgia Capitol Museum.

Samuel Parks: Mutzi's first and only true love and her late-in-life husband. Retired Army Chaplain.

Leroy Dickens: Dahlonega Health Inspector.

George Ledbetter: Marge's deceased husband. He built their large Victorian house, and his spirit often serves as a sounding board for Marge when she needs advice.

Thelma Martin: Owner of Magical Threads and the local

town gossiper.

Ashley McDougal: A soon to graduate college student living with Marge and soon to be co-manager of the Skipping Stone Lodge.

Reverend Mitch Boyen: Pastor of St. Paul the Apostle Church and a special friend to Mutzi.

Jack Hooks: Dahlonega Sheriff and friend of Marge.

Chapter One

This new ensemble was even more radical than the orange jumpsuit Chuck Hansen had been forced to wear what seemed like only a heartbeat ago. He studied himself in the full-length mirror outside the changing room of J. R. Crider's. The cobalt blue crew-neck shirt, brown blazer, and slim dungarees snugged his aging but muscular body tighter than the Consolidated Gold Mine staff shirt and khakis he had worn into the store.

The reflection of Sandi Jackson smiling at him from across the room encouraged a smirk from Chuck. He swore the lights in every room brightened in Sandi's presence.

Her sleeveless stark-white linen blouse—cropped just short of her slender waistline—enhanced her toned bronze arms and provided a pleasant distraction to the sullen mood he'd been in when she'd forced him to go shopping for a new wardrobe.

Although she owned an exquisite Atlanta boutique which carried an impressive line of men's fashions, she'd thoughtfully offered to meet him in Dahlonega in order to save a few hours in his time-crunched schedule.

"Looking good." She winked and held up a wine-colored cable-knit sweater. "Try this one next."

He trusted this woman—the one worthy of being featured on the cover of *Ebony*—to make selections for his new role as a proprietor of Skipping Stone Lodge. He also admired her internal beauty that shined as bright as a one-hundred-watt bulb.

Known throughout the state as a successful entrepreneur, she generously provided support for struggling businesses to keep them afloat when COVID took its toll on the economy.

She'd been quick to support Chuck's proposal for opening a lodge on the outskirts of town. "Not just any lodge," she'd suggested. "It should be a healing safe haven for people with troubled hearts where they'll find comfort, support, and a new perspective."

The idea resonated with Chuck, and he jumped at the chance to buy an abandoned property. Even with Sandi's continued encouragement, his enthusiasm waned with each challenge he faced. Success wasn't meant for people like him.

Low self-esteem—Chuck's Achilles heel. He fought it every hour of every day. Like a scratched forty-five record, powerful painful words from his childhood repeated in his head whenever a prideful accomplishment offered to boost his ego.

Who the hell do you think you are? You're nobody. You always will be.

Another glimpse in the mirror produced a guttural sigh. The two-inch scar above his right eye pulled him to the dark reminder of the incarceration that stole so much of his life. The ugly blemish of being a convicted felon—guilty or not—clung to him like a dark shadow.

Sandi drew closer and hip bumped him. "Don't."

"What?" He pressed a hand across his mouth and rubbed his chin in an attempt to somehow block the exposed negative thoughts.

"Don't go there. Guilt and self-reproach are for losers. You, Chuck Hansen, are not a loser."

He looked away and drew in a slow, deep breath, trying to dispel the angst boiling inside. There were so many hurdles to jump before the opening of the lodge. If he stumbled, even once, it could mean failure. Doubt intensified with each hour as deadlines neared. "But what if—"

"No! No what ifs." Her timbre commanded his full attention. "Focus on where you are now, what you've accomplished, not where you've been. You've got this."

Did he? He wanted to believe achieving this outrageous endeavor would prove to himself and others that he was worthy of...what? Being a productive citizen in the community? Having accomplished a positive achievement? Earning a reputation for helping others who are struggling?

That last one was what this journey had been about to him. Sandi helped him see the possibilities, offered financial support, and urged his sisters to join him on the journey. The end...no...the inaugural ceremony just days away.

Skipping Stone Lodge shined, the result of a year of planning the details, meeting with city officials for permits, and back-breaking work refurbishing the forsaken complex. Chuck had stayed within budget by making most of the repairs himself, but the unexpected expenses for the new heating and cooling system and refrigeration unit had depleted his contingency fund.

Exhaustion at the end of each day limited the time Chuck spent worrying about what else could go wrong. Guests were booked for Thanksgiving and Christmas, but depending on how they rated their experiences, who knew about next year. With the first installment on his loan due in January, the fear of bankruptcy increased tenfold. Failure would not only reinforce the loser identity he tried so hard to shed, but it also meant disappointing the sisters who had worked hard right along with him.

Sandi glared, a silent warning to respond to her words. He gave a cautious nod. "Right. *We've* got this." For the next two weeks, he needed to listen to her advice and focus on what *has* been done. Two permits away. His gaze remained on Sandi's always confident face.

"Thank you." He drew in a deep breath. "For your endless support. And your friendship."

She shrugged and thumbed through another rack of clothing. "No need."

"Yes. There is. None of this would have been possible without your help. I would still be staring at the for-sale sign, dreaming of a way to buy that property."

He grasped her hand. "I've never believed in miracles...at least not until Sam rescued me from living in my car and brought me to Dahlonega. I didn't trust him or anyone, but he offered me a chance to get off the street. Something compelled me to accept his offer. I never truly imagined I could live a normal life and earn a living.

"Prison sucked what little hope I held for my future. The only reason I earned my degree was to fill the long, boring hours. I never believed I'd be able to use the knowledge to own my own business. You showing up at the realty company that day, talking with me, and seeing potential—that was another miracle."

"Everything happens for a reason." She offered a shrug. "It was meant to be. Call it a miracle or whatever, a higher power brought us together."

"A higher power, indeed." He nodded. "But I'm grateful to you for putting your trust in me even with all my baggage."

"I followed my instincts. Besides, I did it for your sister, too. Marge is my best friend. She'd always talked about opening a bed and breakfast. I couldn't pass up the opportunity to help make her dream come true. Like I said, it was meant to be."

Perhaps she was right. Some things were not to be questioned. The mention of Marge's name triggered another proof of how unexpected good fortunes had changed his life. If he hadn't agreed to give a sample of his blood while in prison and Marge hadn't decided to test her DNA, he might never have learned he had three sisters.

Chuck took the burgundy sweater offered to him. "So, I guess you're going to make me buy this too?"

"Probably. Try it on."

He slipped off the blazer, handed it to her, and pulled the sweater over his head. The eye roll from Sandi did not go unnoticed.

"What? It fits. Right?"

"They make dressing rooms for that." She shifted the clothes hanging on her arm from one side to the other.

He tugged at the hem and adjusted the sleeves. "I've gained a couple pounds sampling all the recipes Marge tried out for the grand opening."

"You can afford it."

With Sandi's nod of approval, he released a sigh. "Speaking of food, can we go now? I'm hungry. It's way past lunchtime."

She laughed. "You're always hungry. Get changed."

Avoiding another reprimand from her, Chuck walked into the dressing room and slipped back into his work clothes. When he came out, Sandi handed the new wardrobe to him.

"I'll go across the street to the diner and get us a table while you check out. Meet you there."

The total on the register made him cringe. *Did he really need all of these clothes?* "She'd notice if I put a few back," he muttered to himself, then took the bags to his truck, and hurried to the restaurant where a long line of diners waited to be seated. Moving past them, he found Sandi in a booth by the window.

As he eased onto the bench across from her, a man at a nearby table glared in his direction. Chuck picked up his napkin and tried to ignore the stare.

"Not sure what that guy's problem is."

Sandi shrugged and took a sip of her water. "Who knows. Maybe he's having a bad day."

When the waitress walked past, the guy stopped her and mumbled something. Her head snapped toward Chuck and she shook her head. "This is the only table available right now."

The woman sitting with the grumpy customer frowned. "What's wrong with you, Jasper? Stop being so foolish."

With a loud harrumph, he slammed down the menu.

"I'm not sitting next to him. That lowlife should have been hung."

The words rattled through Chuck's brain and settled in his stomach. It wasn't the first time he'd been through this. Folks in Dahlonega knew of his stint in prison. Even though the murder conviction had been overturned, some people still held him responsible, especially after his second false arrest.

Some things would never change. How could he have ever convinced himself they would? The tabloids always managed to plaster the face of a person arrested for a crime on the front page. When mistakes were made, the accused victim, if he or she was lucky, might merit a line or two correcting the misconception buried next to a want ad.

The woman continued to reprimand her lunch partner loud enough for Chuck to hear. "Stop. You're embarrassing me." Her eyes met Chuck's and she mouthed a "sorry," before she glared at the man across from her. "They found him not guilty. He's innocent. You know that."

"He might have convinced a judge, but anyone who gets caught in a mess like that twice is guilty in my book."

Chuck stood and placed his napkin on the table. "I can't do this, Sandi. I'm sorry. I'll wait for you outside." With a clenched jaw, he trudged to his truck.

What had he been thinking? Sure, some of the folks in town had warmed to him, but there would always be the handful of people who would not accept his innocence. How could he possibly have thought owning a lodge would erase his stained reputation?

He paced on the sidewalk wrought between anger and despair. A few minutes later, the restaurant door opened and Sandi walked out.

"That was awful. I gave him a piece of my mind." She placed a hand on Chuck's arm.

Cold fury overwhelmed him. He gritted his teeth and said, "I'm sorry. You shouldn't have to hear that crap."

"There's nothing for you to be sorry about, Chuck. He's the one with the problem, not you. You didn't kill that woman and you didn't hurt the girl at the mine. In both cases, you were a victim, not a villain."

Chuck studied her sincere face. Her reputation throughout all of Georgia was that of a successful, brilliant business woman. She'd opened and managed multiple stores. Dragging her into his problems had never entered his mind when she offered to help finance the opening of the lodge. And yet, here she was, not only having lunch with a former convict, but investing in his future.

"Look, Sandi. You've been a generous and supportive friend, but you don't need someone like me casting negative shadows—"

"Chuck Hansen, don't you dare bail on me." Fire burned in her eyes. She punched his shoulder. "We are two weeks away from opening the lodge. I need you to block out whatever negative talk is going on inside that handsome head of yours. Right now!"

Her words landed with the force of a boulder. She was right. Backing out now would cause irreparable damage. He'd not only be letting her down, but his sisters, too. So much effort had gone into this adventure, they'd all disown him, and nothing, absolutely nothing, was worth that.

He swallowed hard and nodded. "No bailing. Promise."

She rubbed his arm where she'd smacked him, sending bolts of electricity through his body. Damn this woman. Not only could she read his mind, but her touch sent him to places he fought hard to resist. A hint of a smile forced its way to his lips. *She thinks I'm handsome? This incredible woman thinks I'm handsome.*

With renewed determination, he straightened. "I'm starved. How about you?"

"Heck, yah." She grinned.

He took her hand and led them back into the diner.

Chapter Two

Marge Ledbetter woke at five a.m. and couldn't go back to sleep. She'd decided to drive to the lodge and get some baking done early. A hint of the morning sun filtered through thick woods as she placed the last tray of cookies into the oven and set the timer.

Through the kitchen window, she noticed an unfamiliar white van pull close to the back door of the lodge. She brushed a little flour from her blue gingham apron, glanced at her reflection in the microwave, and walked toward the calendar hanging on the wall. "Hmm. No deliveries or repairmen are scheduled for today." Talking to herself out loud was a habit she'd developed a decade ago. She eased closer to the door, inched the curtain back a smidge, and peeked out.

A curl of salt and pepper hair dipped over the left eye of the man who fastened a tool belt around his waist. "Just like the one George used to wear." He wasn't quite as handsome as her deceased husband, but he certainly was easy on the eyes. She watched him remove a clipboard from the front seat and walk toward the door.

She rested a hand on the knob, waiting for his knock. The door flew open and Marge tumbled forward with a yelp. Her arms flung straight out to brace a fall and she stopped abruptly against the man's solid chest.

"For goodness sakes." Heat crept up her neck and settled in her cheeks. She stepped back and folded her arms tight across her bosom. "Didn't your mother teach you any manners?"

The man fumbled with his clipboard and dropped his pen. He bent to pick it up and smacked his head on a large commercial can opener bolted to the wall near the door. Thick unruly brows drew tight as he rubbed the crown of his head. "The instructions said to come in through the unlocked door at the back entrance"

"Well, you found the right door, but most courteous folks knock before charging in and scaring the daylights out of a person." She hurried across the room, grabbed a couple ice cubes from the freezer, tucked them in a dishcloth, and handed it to him. "Here. Hold this on your head."

With a slight hesitation and another frown, he accepted her offer.

"There's no one on our work schedule today. Who are you?" Marge made a mental note to argue against Chuck's decision to leave the back door unlocked for repairmen.

The fellow pressed his lips tight and cringed as if she'd stepped on a sore toe.

"Leroy Dickens. Food Service Inspector." Shuffling from one foot to the other, he grumbled, "I didn't think anyone was here."

The oven timer dinged. Marge picked up a mitt and moved toward the stove.

"You've got something baking in there?"

"As if you couldn't smell the cinnamon." She scoffed. "Snickerdoodles. Why?"

With a quick glance at his watch and another harrumph, he added. "Throws off my schedule. Can't assess with a hot oven." An exaggerated sigh followed. "I'll work around it."

"These are my husband's favorite." George had been gone a dozen years but the inspector didn't need to know it. Being alone in a remote location justified misleading him—or was it a little white lie—either way, she'd ask for forgiveness during confession on Friday.

He placed the ice pack in the sink and headed toward the walk-in freezer. "Hair restraints are required. And proper shoes."

An instinctive apology hesitated on her mind, then dissipated with the irritation of his sharp tone. "I am not cooking for guests today. I'm merely testing some recipes."

Marge nibbled her bottom lip. She needed to ease the tension between them. Spiteful words might lead to a failed inspection they couldn't afford. Another glance at the microwave confirmed her chin length brown hair, the color of aged mahogany, remained unscathed.

"There's no thermometers in this freezer." He slammed the door and tugged on it, then made a note on his paperwork.

Flustered at his abruptness, but intent on keeping the peace, she said, "Thanks for the reminder." She returned to the stove. Using a spatula, she lifted the cookies from the sheet and placed them on a cooling rack.

"You weren't supposed to be here until next week."

"I'm old school. Do things my way. On my schedule. Got a problem with it, file a complaint with city hall. That'll probably set you back another three months."

The baking sheet banged as Marge tossed it into the deep sink with a little more force than normal. She'd restrained herself from throwing the oven mitt at the inspector, but he pushed her buttons. Only once had she resorted to such childish behavior. A few years ago, she'd thrown a towel at her sister, Rose Ellen. The first and only time in sixty-five years she'd been riled enough to resort to such inappropriate action. Father Mitch actually laughed when she admitted it had felt good.

Leroy continued his examination of the refrigerator, exhaust hood, storage units, and every inch of the kitchen. Marge watched as he methodically checked each area and made annotations on the form. If he hadn't been so surly, he'd have reminded her of George. They were similar in size and probably age. If only he'd smile. She considered offering him cookies and perhaps a cup of coffee. Maybe she should. A little kindness is probably what he needed.

"Would you like a few cookies and a hot cup of coffee or tea?"

Instead of the smile she'd hoped for, his face hardened. "Are you trying to bribe me?"

The suggestion infuriated her more. "For goodness sakes. What is wrong with you? I was trying to be polite."

He tore the sheet off his pad and laid it on the counter. For a brief moment, he gazed at her, then turned to leave. His voice barely audible, he added, "I'll be back next week." He tapped the paper. "These things need to be fixed by then." The door banged behind him.

"I bet he's a widower." The pain in his dark chocolate eyes hadn't escaped Marge's attention. She'd recognized it many times over the years. The sorrow. The emptiness. The open wound which never seems to heal.

Women cry without shame. They fill the void with food, volunteering, or spending money. For men, it's harder. They're forced to hide their tears, turning to brown bottles or wrapping themselves in thorns so no one can get close enough to see their scars.

Marge lifted the inspection checklist and read the note typed on the bottom of the form. *This is an unofficial* **pre-check** *of your facility. It is offered* **without charge** *in advance so you have time to correct any issues that will not pass inspection.*

Tough as nails on the outside. She suspected a kind heart hid inside that leathery facade. This pre-check was exactly the kind of thing George did when he was alive. Always thinking ahead. Always trying to make someone's burdens lighter.

"What a lovely gesture, Leroy," she muttered out loud.

"Who's Leroy?"

Startled by Chuck's voice, she dropped the paper and it floated across the room. "Our health inspector. He showed up a week early."

Chuck snatched the sheet before it hit the floor and read the list. "You must have smooth-talked him with some of those cookies. This list is pretty minimal."

Marge folded her arms. "We didn't exactly hit it off. He was all business." She paused, then added, "He refused my cookies. Thought they were a bribe."

The suggestion brought a hearty laugh from Chuck. "He sure picked the wrong sister for that assumption. I'll make sure to be here next week when he returns and set him straight."

With a stomp of her foot, Marge declared, "You'll do no such thing! I can fight my own battles."

Chuck threw his hands up and smiled. "No brotherly intervention. Got it."

Her cell phone rang. Marge pulled it from her pocket and looked at the caller ID. She swiped the screen. "Oh, my gosh. I'm sorry! I forgot! I'm on my way." She ended the call and whipped off her apron.

Chuck tipped his head to the side. "What'd you forget?"

She hurried to the pantry for an empty container. "I'm supposed to meet some of the members of the Woman's Club to shop for items for the auction baskets."

"For the Christmas Market?"

"Yes. We started months ago, but we need more supplies." Marge hurried to put the cookies in the tin.

"Let me do that." He took the container and began filling it. "Be careful driving."

"You're a dear. Thanks." She checked her hair in the hall mirror and applied a fresh coat of lipstick. "I'll see you tomorrow morning. No. Make that afternoon. I have a meeting in the morning with the Lumpkin County Library about sponsoring the children's program."

Chuck stepped in her path. "Marge. Slow down. You don't have to be here every day."

"But—"

"No buts. You're spreading yourself too thin."

She pecked his cheek. "A promise is a promise." With keys swaying in her hand, she dashed around him. "I have to go. We'll talk later."

The kitchen door banged behind her as she headed to the car. "I need to remind Chuck to fix that." She tugged at the seatbelt and struggled to snap it into place. "Ugh!" Finally on the road, she massaged her neck with one hand as she drove and mentally reviewed the week's schedule. Every hour of every day was filled with commitments. "Please, George. Help remind me. I can't afford to forget another thing,"

She gripped the steering wheel so tight her wrist ached. A glance at the speedometer reminded her to slow down as a series of turns through the thick woods neared. Deer had been known to travel this part of town and a car crash would truly put her in a pickle. Besides, she reasoned, some women in the club were frequently late. Just this once, it was her turn. Surely, they'd forgive her.

Away from the forested area, the radio sputtered to life. A song ended and the announcer chirped, "Only thirty-nine more shopping days until Christmas."

Marge's screech shook the car windows.

Chapter Three

With his last day of work at the Consolidated Gold Mine behind him, Chuck had moved all his belongings into one of the twelve bedrooms at the lodge. The first night, rain pelted the roof with relentless abandon. A gut feeling urged him from the bed to the couch in the great room to keep an eye on the half-dollar-sized discolored circle on the ceiling near the fireplace. His four-legged faithful companion, Shadow, circled around until he found the perfect position on the floor nearby.

Replacing the roof wasn't possible at this point. He'd budgeted for the upgrade of the plumbing and wiring throughout the place, but not the extensive termite-damage which required repair. The decision to accept the property at a reduced price provided he didn't ask for an inspection no longer seemed wise.

He monitored the leak until midnight when the rain stopped. Unable to keep his eyes open any longer, he dozed off. The alarm clock woke him at dawn and he pulled the blanket tight. A splat of dripping water found his ears. Bolting from the couch, he felt cold liquid seep into his sock as his foot slid and he thudded to the floor.

"Aw, for crying out loud!"

Shadow whined and squirmed next to him, apparently unsure how to help. Chuck stared at the steady drip from the now plate-size spot on the ceiling. Drops bounced off the recently refinished hardwood floor. He struggled to his feet and limped to the kitchen for a bucket, mop, and towels, cursing under his breath as he hurried back to begin damage control.

Disgust twisted in his empty stomach. "Why? Why now?" He paced, wracking his brain for some spark of a chance this new hurdle wouldn't break him. Much like his depleted contingency budget, his emotional bank was also overdrawn.

The foolish adventure of opening the lodge had started when Marge shared her dream of running a bed and breakfast. The brittle, corner-curled sale flyer for the rustic resort had hung for months, perhaps years, in the realty company's window. The dream grew into a passion and the possibility of restoring it seemed like the perfect opportunity to give back to his sisters for their love and support. At the same time, he'd hoped to build a new image of himself in the community.

Although Marge and Mutzi had not invested financially, they had devoted months to sweeping, scrubbing, and promoting the project. Thank goodness Rose Ellen had decided not to be involved. It was bad enough to think he'd failed two of his sisters if he didn't succeed.

As his partner, Sandi had invested all she could afford. Chuck was tapped out. There was no access to the thousands more he'd need for a new roof, and they couldn't open with it leaking.

He needed to cancel, or at least postpone the grand opening. Breaking the news to Marge and Mutzi would be tough, but it had to be done. He collapsed onto a chair, pulled out his phone, and dialed.

Sun broke through the clouds by late afternoon. Chuck had done the best he could to clean up the mess. A thorough check of the dining hall, kitchen, and bedrooms revealed the leak had only been in the great room. To expend the anxiety brewing in his gut, he'd worked on the list of repairs the inspector had left. Marge had insisted on it when he'd called her, although there didn't seem to be an urgency anymore.

The crunch of gravel drew his attention to the window. Mutzi's red pickup rolled up the driveway with his other sisters on board. He trudged outside and offered a hand to Rose Ellen as she scooted out the passenger door. Marge exited the back seat without his assistance. Shadow galloped toward Mutzi as she walked around the truck. Chuck's eccentric, silly sister often teased him that Shadow belonged to her, even though Mutzi had her own lab named Midnight.

A lump formed in his throat as he looked at his three siblings. "I—I wasn't expecting all of you to come. There's really nothing you can do."

"The Dahlonega Sisters to the rescue." Mutzi nudged him with her elbow. "You should know by now we don't give up without a fight."

He hadn't known, or at least hadn't expected his relatively new family to step up and bail him out...again. Most of his troubled life, he'd battled alone, unaware he had siblings. Verbal and physical abuse from his adoptive father left him fractured, bouncing from town to town, job to job, believing he wasn't worthy of more. The only person who ever offered kind words was his mother, and she'd passed when he was five.

Was there really something his sisters could do?

Marge walked toward the front entrance of the lodge with Mutzi and Shadow on her heels. "Let's go inside and see what we're dealing with."

Chuck held the door and waited for Rose Ellen to follow.

She paused, seemingly fascinated with the elaborate scroll carvings on the frame. With a nod, she stated, "Striking woodwork. Makes an appealing entry."

Surprised at the compliment, Chuck smiled. "You've been here before, haven't you?" He remembered her harsh criticism when he bought the place. Rose Ellen often voiced her opinion without any filters.

"Yes. Once." She withdrew a notebook from her purse and jotted something down before going inside.

Mutzi snapped a picture of the two as they came through the door.

The flash blinded Chuck for a moment, the burst of light a painful reminder of reporters who captured photos when he was dragged from the mine in handcuffs. "Not today, Sis. Maybe Shadow would like his picture taken."

"I already took a dozen of him." She stroked the black lab's fur. "He still likes me better."

Chuck rolled his eyes. "He does enjoy your company, for sure."

Marge stared at the ceiling. "Another speed bump. Such a shame. Things were going so well."

Speed bump? Doesn't she get how serious this is?

"Who wants some tea?" With a shrug of her shoulders, Marge headed to the kitchen.

Chuck shook his head, unsure whether to be relieved or upset. He'd stressed all day about how she'd take the news. "I don't get it, Marge. I thought you'd be distraught. This could be the breaking point for opening the lodge."

She smiled. "Problems are unresolved opportunities. Roofs are fixable. We'll find a way."

Rose Ellen gave the ceiling a quick glance. "She's right. There's always a way." She tugged on Marge's arm. "Let's go get that tea. I've got some great ideas for sprucing this place up."

Marge yanked her arm away. "Sprucing it up? What do you think we've been doing for months?"

"Oh, you've done a nice job. I see lots of improvements." She moved close to the picture window and ran a hand down the drapes. "I bet you made these. They are lovely."

The compliment did not ease Marge's pursed lips. She marched into the kitchen without responding. Rose Ellen followed.

Chuck chose to stay in the great room away from the anticipated confrontation. His sisters barking at each other might raise his anxieties to an unmanageable level.

A smirk spread across Mutzi's face. "Oh, boy. They're at it already."

Rubbing his hands together, Chuck looked for a distraction from the bickering sisters. "I think it's time to start a fire."

Mutzi slapped her leg and laughed. "You should be used to our sister-fussing by now."

"Makes me more tense and my nerves are shot already." He arranged a few logs and lit them.

With her hands pressed together, Mutzi giggled and bowed. "Namaste. Want me to show you how to meditate?"

The ridiculous suggestion made him laugh. "Thanks, but there aren't enough hours in the day as it is."

She patted him on the back. "Ease up, bro. We'll get past this and laugh about it later."

"Wish I had your confidence." *Same thing I said to Sandi. Need to work on that.* "I like the bro thing."

Mutzi shrugged. "Me too. Always wanted a brother."

Chuck wrapped an arm around her. "I'm blessed to have you gals as sisters. Truly blessed." He'd believed he was an only child for sixty-plus years. While in prison, he'd agreed to genetic testing as proof of his innocence. He'd never anticipated how it could change his life in other ways, too.

Once the kettle whistled and drinks were served, each of them chose one of the overstuffed loungers Chuck had arranged in a semicircle near the hearth.

With a sigh, he began, "Here's the situation." Sparing no details, he reviewed the itemized repairs and expenses. "I've surpassed my budget with no other options to pay for the roof. The well is dry."

Marge spoke first. "I could mortgage my Victorian."

He shook his head. "Don't even consider it. There's no way I would let you do that."

"I'd give you money if I had it," Mutzi added. "You know that."

"I know you would. Thanks." He rubbed the pulse pounding in his temple. This was going nowhere, as he'd half expected.

Rose Ellen leaned forward. With her elbow on the arm of the chair, she propped her chin on her fist. "I have a proposition. I want to be an investor. I'll give you whatever you need to get this place open."

All eyes shifted to her.

The words dangled like a fistful of crisp bills. "An investor?" Chuck's breath caught, and then he slowly released it. "What would that involve?"

Rose Ellen shifted in her seat and folded her arms.

"You need money. I have money at my disposal. I'll loan you what you need for the roof repairs and any additional unexpected expenses. Simple as that."

"I don't know when I'd be able to pay you back."

"I understand the situation. I can wait."

Chuck rubbed his chin and considered the generous offer. The proposal should have made him jump for joy. Instead, the knot in his belly clenched tighter. He'd become close with Marge and Mutzi. Their personalities blended well with his. Rose Ellen not so much. Her intentions sometimes were questionable and her explanations often filled with missing details and half-truths. He didn't want to offend her, and for now, she was his only hope.

He mulled over the past few years. When his truck had been destroyed by fire, she'd generously bought him an expensive new one—with more add-ons than he'd ever need—and pretended she could afford it when in reality, she'd taken out a loan to pay for it. She constantly spent money to the point of bankruptcy just to impress others. Although her monetary situation significantly changed when she married Roberto, Chuck wondered if her husband knew of her current offer to invest in the lodge.

Another nagging concern weighed on him. He had to ask. "What's in it for you, Rose Ellen?"

She smiled and said, "I want to be part of the adventure."

Chuck glanced toward Marge who was wringing her hands. *Is she anxious for me to agree or concerned I'll take the offer?*

A drop of water plopped into the bucket. The urgency of the situation badgered him. He wished for more time to consider his decision. Truth was, there wasn't any. The chance a roofing company could squeeze the lodge into their schedule in time was slim. A second drop splashed.

With an extended hand, Chuck shook on the deal. "I'll call roofing companies today."

A sly grin spread across Rose Ellen's face. "Send me an email with the choices and I'll pick which one I like best."

Regret slid down Chuck's spine.

Chapter Four

T he three sisters said goodbye to Chuck and climbed into the truck.

About a mile down the road, Mutzi tilted the rear-view mirror enough to make eye contact with Rose Ellen who sat behind her in the back seat. She'd sensed her oldest sister had a hidden motive for offering help. "So, what's the catch?"

Rose Ellen adjusted the cashmere cardigan around her shoulders before responding. "I don't know what you mean."

"Baloney. You know exactly what I mean. Like Chuck asked, what's in it for you?"

"I'm offended you think there's a catch."

Mutzi shot a quick glance at Marge, knowing she'd be uncomfortable with Mutzi for stirring the proverbial pot, especially since Marge and Rose Ellen had been squabbling earlier. To her surprise, Marge was staring at Rose Ellen and chimed in.

"I'm sure Chuck appreciated your offer. But I'm curious, too. What changed your mind? You didn't want anything to do with the lodge until now."

Rose Ellen crossed her arms. "We're family. I want to help my brother."

The answer didn't satisfy Mutzi. She pushed, "And?"

"Well, if this lodge thing is successful, I'd like my name associated with it."

Marge grew impatient. "Why now?"

Mutzi snarled. "The hard work's almost done, and now she wants to take credit for it."

Rose Ellen poked Mutzi's shoulder. "That's not true. If you remember correctly, last year I became a curator's wife when I married Roberto. The position came with significant expectations, like fund raisers, banquets, and other important events you wouldn't know about." She took a breath and continued, "Besides, after our extended honeymoon in Europe, I had to supervise the massive remodel of our house. I didn't have time to help clean the mess at the lodge, too."

The exhaustive explanation ended the inquisition. They rode in silence the rest of the way to Marge's house.

As her two sisters climbed out of the truck, Mutzi said, "Have a good night, Marge. Be careful driving home, Rose Ellen."

A defiant glare covered Rose Ellen's face. "I'm not driving to Atlanta tonight. I'm staying at Marge's."

The wide-eyed reaction from Marge made it clear it was the first she'd heard of the plan. Mutzi chuckled to herself and waved as she drove away.

"Alexa. Call home." Of all the electronic accessories available in today's vehicles, she appreciated the hands-free phone option the most. Well, that, and the park assist. Not having to maneuver into tight parking spots was great, too. The home phone rang until the recorded voice spoke.

"Damn it. He's late getting home again." She ended the call without leaving a message. "Time to talk with Father Mitch."

Marge fumed as she climbed the unlit porch steps, muttering through clenched teeth, "You could use a refresher course in manners." Once on the landing, she watched Rose Ellen stroll to her car, pull out an overnight bag from the trunk, plunk it on the ground, and wait.

A tinge of guilt for not helping her older sister with her luggage like she normally would, surfaced briefly. Marge ignored it, turned, and fumbled while trying to put her key into the lock.

From the street, Rose Ellen called out. "You should leave the porch light on when you're going to be out late."

Marge chewed her bottom lip and sucked in a deep breath. "I'll try to remember that next time."

Once inside, she flipped on the outside light, dropped her purse on the foyer table, and turned on a lamp. Her sister's unnecessary reminder that she'd forgotten one more thing irritated her. Exhausted from bickering with Rose Ellen, she made her way into the kitchen and put a kettle on the stove.

The front door opened with a whack and Marge tensed. It took all of her patience not to shout at Rose Ellen for banging the wall. Instead, she listened as Rose Ellen rolled her overnight bag down the hall to the room she occasionally stayed in.

Just as the kettle whistled, her sister appeared in the kitchen.

"I don't suppose you have purple tea? I've become quite fond of it, but it's hard to find and more expensive than the brands you usually have."

The muscles in Marge's neck tightened. Massaging it with her hand no longer helped, so she reached into the cabinet for ibuprofen. "I don't have purple tea. You'll have to force yourself to settle for my simple chamomile tonight."

Marge filled two mugs and placed them on the island. "Did you let Roberto know you were spending the night?"

"Of course. I told him before I left." Rose Ellen eased onto a stool.

"It would've been nice if you'd told me, too." Marge rolled her shoulders.

"Why bother? I knew you'd say yes."

Let it go. It's late. Don't say something you'll regret. "You're right. I'd never turn anyone away." The Victorian was already too empty with just her and Ashley. Her college boarder would graduate soon, and Marge worried about being alone again if the young woman decided to move out.

Rose Ellen sipped her tea and set the cup down. "I have some exciting plans for the lodge. Want to hear them?"

"Plans? You do realize we have planned for nearly a year. Things are just the way we want them."

She shrugged. "It should be more upscale. Not so rustic."

"It's a lodge—in the woods—by a river. It's supposed to be rustic."

"Why can't we appeal to a—now don't get mad—a higher class of people. We should offer luxury spa treatments and perhaps some sort of entertainment. No one I know would stay there the way it is."

There it was. The reason Rose Ellen wanted to be an investor. Bragging rights to her snooty friends. *Time to bring my older sister down to earth.*

"Skipping Stone Lodge is a place for people to come to heal. Whether it's a person grieving from the loss of a loved one, hurt from a failed relationship, or desperately in need of a fresh start, we'll offer them a place to relax, an ear to listen—if and when they want to share—and a chance to release the burdens they've been carrying."

Rose Ellen pursed her lips. "Quite commendable, but will it be profitable?" She drained her cup and set it down. "People with money have issues too, you know. We could charge more, and they'd be willing to pay—if we offer the right amenities." She stood and moved toward the hall.

Marge stepped in front of her. "Put your cup in the dishwasher. I am not your servant. Goodnight." Then Marge walked out without looking back.

Chapter Five

When the doors opened at Moore's Lumber & Hardware store, Chuck was the first customer to enter. With a list of needed items, he trudged through the aisles and gathered clamps, extra thermometers, and a razor knife. As he headed toward the checkout, a man with "RRG Roofing" on his pocket strolled past him.

Chuck called out to him, "Hey, mister. Got a minute?"

The fellow slowed and turned. "Me? What's up?"

"I noticed your shirt. I'm scheduled to open a lodge in two weeks and I really need a roofer. I woke this morning to a big puddle in the great room near the fireplace. Any chance—"

"The old Lambert Lodge?" The man's eyes lit and a half-grin pulled at his cheek. "Loved that place. I heard somebody bought it."

"That's the one. It's been an uphill battle, but we're close to the end—at least I thought we were—until this roof issue. The repairs are about to put me in the poor-house."

The guy tilted his head and drew his brows tight. "I put the roof on that building a few years before it shut down. Surprised it's leaking."

"Me, too. It looked like it was in good shape. Any chance you could take a look at it?" Chuck held his breath, hoping for another miracle.

"I'm swamped today, but I'll try to squeeze you in to-morrow." He reached into his pocket and pulled out a business card. "The name's Rudy."

"Chuck Hansen." He fumbled with his wallet for the card Mutzi insisted he would need someday. "My num-ber's on there."

Rudy held the card away from him as far as his arm could reach and then withdrew a pair of readers. "Skip-ping Stone Lodge. Catchy name. Bet there's a great story behind it but..." with a quick glance at his watch, he added, "I don't have time to hear it right now. I'll be in touch."

The unexpected interaction re-energized Chuck. If Mutzi had been there, she'd say running into Rudy was serendipity. In his mind, it was more than that. *Thank you, Lord.*

With more pep in his step, he paid for his items and walked outside. Replaying the conversation with Rudy,

Chuck almost stumbled over someone sitting on the curb with his head in his hands. "Whoa. Didn't see you there. Sorry."

A gaunt face looked up, absent of emotion. The guy, perhaps early twenties, appeared to be down on his luck. Torn jeans, the hems of each leg ragged from dragging the ground. Dusty brown hair hung past the neckline of his wrinkled, holey t-shirt, and dangled near his dimpled chin.

Wasn't long ago when Chuck wore the same type of faded, frayed jeans and torn shirt. He settled next to the kid. "Rough day?"

The young man drew his arms tight around his knees.

How can I reach him? A few years ago, when Chuck was homeless, Mutzi's husband, Sam, had approached him and offered a free meal. With a little encouragement, maybe this guy would accept the same offer. "Know any good places to eat around here?"

He glared at Chuck. "What do you think?"

Fair enough. Strike one. He thought some more. "I'm going to that diner over there." Chuck pointed. "You're welcome to join me. My treat."

"What the hell do you want, mister? I don't do drugs, don't know any dealers, and I'm straight as that light pole."

Chuck shrugged. "Wasn't that long ago I was living in my car when a fellow gave me a break. Thought you could use one."

His eyes widened. "You shitting me?"

"Nope. I was on the streets. No family. No place to live. A guy saw me and offered me a chance to get my act together."

Every time Chuck had offered to repay Sam for taking him in, his answer was the same. "Pay it forward." *Is this my chance? What would Mutzi and Marge say?* He knew the answer. They had hearts of gold.

"I'm getting ready to open a lodge. I need an extra hand to help with minor repairs and keeping the grounds trimmed. You game?"

The young man shook his head. "Gotta be a catch. Sounds too good. Stuff like that never happens—at least not to me."

"I remember saying the same thing. But deep down, I've always believed there were good people out there. So, I took a risk. Best decision I ever made." Chuck met the young man's eyes. "Things can change, if you want it bad enough and work hard."

"I'm a hell of a hard worker, but nobody will give me a chance to prove it." His face hardened. "I've been earning money from odd jobs since I was ten. My dad's in and out of jail and my mom skipped town with some dude last year. She took every penny I'd saved when she ran off. Just left me to make it on my own. No place to live. Nothing to eat." As if on cue, his stomach growled. "I can't get a job because I look like a bum. Smell like one too."

"That's a tough life." His story tugged at Chuck's heart. So young. So alone. "Here's the thing. I can't offer you any pay right now. But you'd have a roof over your head and food on the table, if you're willing to take the chance and abide by a few rules."

"I'm listening."

"No drugs. Respect me, my staff...and our guests. In return, I'll respect you." Chuck paused to study the guy's reaction, then continued, "Do what I ask, and be honest. If you agree, you're hired."

"Still sounds fishy, but I ain't getting anywhere sitting here." He rose, wiped his hand on his pants, and raised it in the air. "Buddy Jenkins, at your service."

The grin on his face made Chuck laugh. "Sounds like we've got a deal." He shook Buddy's hand.

"I'm hungry as hell. Is that meal offer still good?"

Chuck nodded and they headed to the diner. Before they stepped inside, Chuck held up a hand. "One more rule. No cussing. My sister Marge doesn't tolerate it. Neither do I. At least not around her."

Buddy paused. "I'll have to work on that one, but I'll try."

Chapter Six

The invitational flyer announcing the grand opening of the lodge had been displayed throughout Dahlonega for a month. More than fifty townsfolk had confirmed they would be there to celebrate. Mutzi also had created an electronic brochure for the Skipping Stone Lodge and advertised it on their new web page. Photos of the alluring Appalachian Mountain acreage that abutted the Chestatee River along with the massive stone fireplace in the Great Room had resulted in a half-dozen reservations for their first "test" week, which began on Thanksgiving Day and ended on the following Monday. That would be enough guests for the first week, but they needed to fill the calendar months ahead in order to make a profit. She decided to print copies on glossy paper to hand out at the grand opening.

Sam called from the kitchen. "Your breakfast is getting cold and I need to leave."

His reminder pricked Mutzi like a thorn. Ever since he'd decided to become a deacon, his tedious training program ruled their days. She pushed away from her desk and marched to the kitchen. Hands on her hips, she barked, "Again? You're leaving again?"

He closed his eyes and sighed. "Honey, you know my schedule."

"You know my schedule," she mimicked with a snarky tone. "Well, I don't like your schedule."

"You supported my decision—our decision—when you were busy with your party planning business and the lodge preparations. Why are you so upset now?"

She dropped her arms to her side. "This house is empty without you...and Chuck. You used to make noise and interrupt me, but I enjoyed having you both underfoot. Ever since Chuck moved out and you've been gone, it's like I don't matter to anyone anymore."

Sam scoffed. "You know you are important to me, hon, but so is being a deacon."

"It doesn't feel like I am. When you do come home, you've got your nose stuck in a book studying."

He pulled her into a hug. "I'm sorry. I am trying."

"You need to try harder. Isn't that what you used to say to me?"

He wrinkled his nose. "Making me eat my own words? Not fair." Planting a quick kiss on her lips, he reached for his leather briefcase. "Now I'm late. See you tonight."

Mutzi grumbled and stomped her foot as her husband walked out, startling the young lab who never left her side. Midnight scooted under the table and stared.

"A lot of help you are. You could have barked or something." She took a piece of bacon from her uneaten breakfast and held it out to him. "Sorry, buddy. I'm not mad at you."

He snatched the meat and swallowed it in a single gulp, then waited for more.

"How about a walk? I think we could both use one." She grabbed his halter, slipped it over his head, and tugged to secure it around his growing body. "Gonna hafta get you a bigger one or stop feeding you my food. Let's go."

As they stepped outside, the sky darkened when black birds circled overhead. Mutzi gasped and pulled her four-legged companion back into the house. "Oh, crap. That's not good."

Her heart raced as she grabbed a chair and clung to it. Standing still didn't slow the trepidation gushing through her veins and settling in her chest with the force of a mac truck. A cold sweat enveloped her body.

Months had passed since the last panic attack. Seeing the foreboding crows triggered long dormant superstitions. The fallacies had ruled her life at one time, but with Sam's help, she'd fought hard to dispel them.

Midnight stayed close, his leash dragging the floor as he followed her every move. She staggered down the hall to her babe cave, the black lab at her heels. With the door closed and blinds shut, she reminded herself to focus on all the textures and scents Sam had incorporated into the room for moments like this.

Picking up a plush, lavender-scented hand towel, she held it to her face and drew a slow, deep breath. Then she moved to the yellow cube bookshelf hanging on the wall and read each title out loud. "*Treasure Island* by Robert Louis Stevenson, *Little Women* by Louisa May Alcott, *Wuthering Heights* by Emily Bronte."

Some people recited the alphabet backward to refocus their attention during an attack. Mutzi preferred reading the titles of her favorite books. She continued pulling classics from the red and green cubes.

She then reversed the process and began putting them back. Once satisfied each had been returned to its original order, she picked up a velvety mint-green pillow and stroked it. The pressure in her chest eased, and her breathing slowed. A hammock that hung in the corner of the room drew her attention, but she chose the rocking chair instead. A flick of a button started the wax flowing in the lava lamp that once had belonged to Sam. With her eyes closed, the rocking helped her find her quiet place.

Visions of the murder of crows circling their house still lingered.

Death or destruction? Which would it be?

Chapter Seven

The morning after staying with Marge, Rose Ellen decided to drive to the lodge before heading back to Atlanta. Chuck had said he would be gone most of the morning and Marge had some commitment with the woman's club, so she'd have the place to herself. She parked close to the front door, got out, and studied the property. Skipping Stone Lodge sat on twenty wooded acres, part of which bordered a peaceful river. Four acacia hardwood rockers graced the rustic front porch, making it tempting for guests to sit a spell.

There wasn't much she could do to add a bit of luxury to the outside. Even the formidable front door met her approval with its hand-hewn mahogany, arched windows, and sidelights.

She remembered Chuck telling Marge the key to the lodge would be hidden in the flowerpot. *Such an obvious place. He should know better.* Still, it worked in her favor today. Inside was where Rose Ellen intended to add her personal touch and give it more allure. Entering the great room, she glanced around. Not bad, but certainly much too rustic to attract the type of clientele she hoped to entertain. She set her Florentine Satchel Dooney & Bourke purse down on the oak side table and dug through it to get a pen and notepad.

First on her list was the much too homey furniture. Plush leather couches and a couple of matching chairs would be more inviting. She'd seen the perfect ensemble in Atlanta, and it came with footstools. The plaid window coverings Marge had made were well-tailored but wouldn't blend with the contemporary Parisian rug she envisioned for the hardwood floor.

She strolled across the room, focused on the built-ins that anchored both sides of the massive stone fireplace. Remington statues would add some richness and provide great conversation pieces. They were pricey but worth the investment.

The rounded pebbled stone fireplace which reached to the ceiling didn't appeal to her taste, but refinishing it before the opening wasn't possible. That was a project for later. She wandered into the dining hall. Built-in shelves along one wall held stacks of exquisitely hand-sewn placemats and napkins. The task of cooking and serving belonged to Marge. So should the room. She turned and walked back out.

The bedrooms were next on her agenda. She'd given it a lot of thought and decided to focus on just one for now. Surely, if Marge or Chuck resisted her ideas, she'd be able to convince them to create one luxury room for special guests.

"Marge did a nice job, don't you think?"

Rose Ellen gasped, and her hand flew to her chest. "You scared the daylights out of me!"

Chuck threw his hands up. "Sorry. I thought you heard me come in. I didn't expect to see you back so soon."

"I was making notes about what I wanted to do in here." She jotted down one word—*everything*.

The comment brought a frown from her brother. "But this room is already finished like Marge wanted it."

Rose Ellen raised a brow and shrugged. "Is she an investor too?" She didn't wait for an answer. "Money talks, and I figure my money entitles me to some control in this place."

Chuck ran a hand through his hair. "We—Marge, Mutzi, and I—have devoted almost a year working on the details. That's a significant investment on all our parts." He drew in a deep breath and released it. "I think we need to discuss what being an investor really means—to all of us."

An inner voice warned Rose Ellen to soften her approach. Even though Chuck needed money, he might find other resources from which to get it. "I'm not planning on changing too many things. Just making the place a little classier to appeal to a wider range of guests. Trust me. It's for the benefit of the lodge." She had her reasons.

"You haven't bought in yet, Rose Ellen. Let's see how much the roof is going to cost. Maybe I won't need—"

Rose Ellen stomped her foot. "You agreed last night. We shook on it." *How dare he try to back out now.*

"Look, Sis, I didn't agree for you to come in and take over." He glanced at his watch. "Marge is coming by this afternoon. Let's discuss it then. For now, I've got repairs in the kitchen that have to get done."

She fumed to herself as he walked away. Why did everyone always resist her ideas? If they'd only listen to reason, they'd understand she did things to benefit them, too.

Her thoughts drifted back to the magnificent Tuscany wedding she'd planned last year. Her family would have enjoyed a lovely, expense-free vacation, and she would have made the front page of Georgia newspapers. But no. Everyone disagreed with her plan. Mutzi wouldn't fly. The date interfered with Marge's commitment to the Gold

Rush Festival. Even Rose Ellen's own daughter, April, complained because she wouldn't look good in a swimsuit while seven months pregnant.

It wasn't that she'd been disappointed with the wedding she and Roberto had. It made the front page of The Dahlonega Gazette. But it could have been so much grander. Surely, her brother and sisters could see the changes she wanted to make to Skipping Stone Lodge were in their best interest, too. It would bring in much more business. She'd find a way to convince them. They'd won the battle about the wedding, but she'd win this one. What was the saying about it's better to ask forgiveness than approval?

With that thought, Rose Ellen called out to Chuck, "I'm leaving." She grabbed her purse and headed home. The sooner she got everything ordered, the sooner she could implement her plan and show them how spectacular the grand opening would be.

Chapter Eight

Chuck jotted a note with a few simple tasks for his new assistant, Buddy. Hang thermometers in the freezer and refrigerator; replace torn screen wire; scrape some frayed liner paper off a pantry shelf and paint it.

The screen door creaked and Chuck looked up. Buddy stood outside, Shadow pressed firm against his leg as if attached by an invisible thread. The dog had taken to the guy. Chuck didn't mind. He had enough to do without entertaining the black Labrador.

"Come on in. I've got some things for you to do." Buddy didn't move. "Is there a problem?"

He glanced down. "My shoes are filthy. I was playing catch with your dog and stepped in some mud."

Chuck rubbed his chin. "What size do you wear?"

The young man shrugged. "I found these in a dumpster."

The tattered, mud-covered shoes looked close to Chuck's size. "Stay there. I'll be right back."

He hurried to his bedroom, grabbed a towel, some socks, and the expensive pair of leather boots he'd worn while working at the mine. Returning to the kitchen, he said. "Put these on."

"You sure? These are kick-ass boots." His eyes widened. "Sorry. I forgot."

Chuck let the curse word slip by since Marge wasn't around.

"They'll have to do until we can get you some that fit."

The guy's eyes focused on the shoes as he stroked the soft socks.

Chuck wondered when the youngster last had a pair of shoes that didn't come from a dumpster or a thrift store. He remembered what it was like to be homeless. He also recalled the pride he felt when he turned over his first paycheck to pay for the Vibram sole boots. Waterproof and durable. They'd been worth it.

"Still not sure why you're being so nice to me. I haven't done anything to deserve it."

The words cut through Chuck's heart. "Everyone deserves the basic essentials. Food, clothing, a roof over their head."

Buddy twisted his mouth but didn't respond. He seemed to be contemplating the idea as if he wasn't convinced it was true. He plopped down on the patio and kicked first one shoe and then the other into the grassy area. The wet socks followed. Using the towel, he dried his feet and slipped on the plush socks and wiggled his toes. "Nice." With the boots laced up, he stood.

"A little big, but they'll keep you warm." Chuck motioned for him to come inside.

"I can stuff some newspaper into the toes. Thanks."

With the scribbled instructions in hand, Chuck pointed to the list. "Think you can tackle these today?"

A grin accompanied Buddy's nod. "As long as you've got a scraper and paint, consider it done."

Great attitude. "How about something to eat first? Marge made a breakfast casserole. It's in the oven."

Buddy's eyes lit with the mention of food. "You bet. I'm starved."

Chuck motioned to the sink. "Important rule. Wash your hands—with soap—whenever you come into the kitchen. Marge is a stickler about cleanliness, and we need to be careful because we'll be feeding guests." Then he showed Buddy where the paper plates and plastic utensils were. "One more rule, clean up after yourself to stay on my sister's good side."

Buddy paused and grew serious. "What's her bad side like?"

That question made Chuck laugh. He tipped his head and thought. "I'm not sure I've seen her bad side, but I bet she's got one. Everyone does."

The conversation ended abruptly when the roar of a diesel engine drew their attention. Chuck walked outside just as the guy from the roofing company climbed from his truck.

"I finished a job a few miles from here and thought I'd stop by to check your roof."

"Great. I really appreciate it."

"The place looks pretty good for being empty for years. Always had fond memories of bringing my wife here on our honeymoon. That was a long time ago." He started unloading a ladder from his truck.

Chuck took one end and helped lean it against the house. "Do you want to go inside and see where the leak is?"

"Nope. You said it's close to the fireplace."

"Right."

"Wind probably tore flashing away from the chimney. With any luck, you might not need a whole new roof."

"Man, that would be the best news I've had in a while."

Chuck held the ladder while Rudy climbed the steps.

"You don't need to do that," he called from the fourth rung. "Been doing this by myself for nearly thirty years."

"Never hurts to have an extra hand, just in case." Chuck considered going up to have a look, but talked himself out of it. He was clueless about repairing roofs. Plus, he wasn't too fond of heights.

Rudy didn't waste any time. He called out as he climbed down the ladder. "This is your lucky day. It's the flashing. I'll have it repaired within the hour."

The weight of a two-ton truck lifted from Chuck's shoulders. He couldn't believe his good fortune. "You have no idea what that means."

"From the look on your face, I think I might." Back on the ground, Ruby walked to his truck. "Go on about your business. I'll let you know when I'm done."

"Thanks." Chuck left to check on Buddy. He stepped through the back door and his mouth dropped open. "Holy crap!"

Buddy froze. "What?"

Every single thing from inside the pantry was piled on the island. If Marge walked in now, she'd probably scream or faint. He wasn't sure which. She had arranged every pie plate, cake pan, and bottle of spice in the exact order she wanted them.

"Um. I appreciate your efforts, Buddy. But only one shelf needed painting." He reprimanded himself. *I need to work on my instructions.*

"I started with that one, but then the other shelves looked dingy, so I decided to paint them all."

Chuck sighed. Buddy was probably right, but how would Chuck ever get everything returned to its original place? "It was my fault." He glanced at the mound of goods, hoping the paint dried fast so he could put the stuff back before Marge got to the lodge. She'd been stressed enough lately. "Next time, check with me first."

Buddy cowered in the corner of the pantry. "I'm really sorry."

Chuck walked over to him and reached out to touch his shoulder. "It's okay. Just a misunderstanding. It's on both of us."

Wary eyes stared back. Buddy remained tucked in the corner, waiting. Chuck sensed the guy's mistakes normally were followed with a beating.

"No one here is going to hurt you. Not on my watch. Trust me."

Buddy paused as if considering whether he could trust Chuck, then turned back to work on the last shelf. "We can start putting things back now. The first shelf is already dry."

Chuck shook his head. "Not yet. It'll need a few more hours."

As luck would have it, the door opened and Marge walked through.

"Oh, my!" She dropped her purse on the counter and turned to Chuck. "What happened?" She dashed to the pantry and looked inside. "Who are you?"

Wide-eyed and splattered with paint, the new hire sputtered, "Buddy. Buddy Jenkins, ma'am." He offered his hand to Marge.

Marge glanced at the paint-covered hand, back to the cluttered island, and then the dam burst. Her shoulders heaved with each sob.

"I'm sorry, ma'am. I'm sorry." Buddy's shoulders slumped.

Even though Chuck had joked about it beforehand, Marge's reaction surprised him. "Let's all take a break." He led her to the couch in the great room. His assistant followed while Shadow squeezed in between the three of them.

After several minutes of silence, Chuck made introductions. "Marge. I didn't have a chance to fill you in. We needed an extra hand around here, and Buddy needed a place to stay."

Marge patted her cheeks with a tissue and offered a weak smile. "I'm sorry for overreacting. I don't usually greet guests that way."

Buddy jumped to his feet. "Oh, I'm not a guest, ma'am. I'm a hired hand—but not for money—for food and a bed."

She rose from the couch, glanced from Chuck back to Buddy, and smiled. "I'll take that handshake now."

He started to extend his hand and then dashed toward the kitchen. When he returned, he offered a damp but clean handshake. "Nice to meet you, ma'am."

"It's Marge. And since you're not a guest, you'll be considered family. Welcome to the clan."

Chapter Nine

The panic attack had exhausted Mutzi, and she'd gone to bed at nine, not even hearing Sam when he came in. She'd woken early the next morning feeling better, but upset with herself for letting the crows trigger an old superstition.

Filled with renewed determination to support her husband in his spiritual efforts, she slipped out of bed and made her way to the kitchen to brew coffee. Midnight followed close behind ready for his morning romp across their six acres. Normally, Sam did most of the cooking, but today Mutzi decided to risk serving him scrambled eggs and toast, pretty confident she wouldn't burn the kitchen down in the process. She knew how to cook, but the smallest thing distracted her.

Sam ambled down the hall, wearing a snappish blue dress shirt and navy pants, his hair still moist from a shower.

"You're up early today, honey. Got big plans?" He pulled her close and planted a kiss on her lips.

She wrapped her arms around his waist and held tight, taking in the woodsy scent of his aftershave. "It's what I have to do to see you." Her tone came out snarkier than she'd intended. "Sorry, I didn't mean it like that."

He stroked her silver hair. "It's okay. I've been gone a lot lately." He kissed her again. "You were asleep when I came in last night. Did you have a busy day with your sisters?"

Not wanting to make Sam feel worse about things, she changed the subject. "We're all meeting at the lodge again today to discuss some issues involving Rose Ellen and her sudden interest in our 'adventure' as she calls it."

"When did she get involved? I thought she was too busy traveling and refurnishing her house."

"The renovations are finished. She's dangling her husband's money as bait in order to be invested." An acrid smell reached her nose. She whipped around and hurried to the stove. "Dang it. Burnt the eggs."

Sam glanced at the pan. "They're salvageable. I'll get the toast."

With the food served, they sat at the table, shoulders almost touching as they ate. It comforted her to have him close. He was such a good man. Always making light of her mistakes and tolerating her misguided ways. The man showed patience beyond reason, never lost his temper, and it took so little effort to please him. She needed to put more effort into supporting him. What really worried her was what would be expected of the deacon's wife once Sam earned the title.

He reached over and squeezed her hand. "I should get done early today. Want to meet in town for dinner?"

"That would be nice. Maybe I'll stop by Marge's on the way back to see if I can help with some of her projects." She glanced at the clock hanging on the wall. "Better get a move on or you'll be late."

He smiled and nodded. "My love. My forever love."

The words always made her close her eyes and feel him in her heart as if they'd become one. She would have liked to stay suspended in the moment, but there was no time. Opening her eyes, and with mock grumpiness, she said, "Enough mushy stuff. We got things to do. Places to go."

She stood, picked up a dish, and with her back turned to him, added, "I love you too, Samuel Parks. Always have. Always will."

He grabbed his briefcase and leaned in for another kiss. Mutzi swatted him on the rear and then followed him onto the porch. He climbed into the truck, and she lingered, watching him drive away. Oh, how she loved that man.

She gathered copies of the brochures she'd been working on and her camera. The thirty-minute drive to the lodge was uneventful. No crows. No black cats. Not even a fox or snake. She did see one owl, but previous research had confirmed they were only bad luck for a mouse.

As she parked, she noticed Chuck and some guy carrying logs to the firepit. Her brother nodded and stacked more wood on a growing pile.

"Marge is inside baking cookies. Haven't seen Rose Ellen yet." He nudged the guy helping him. "This is my sister Mutzi." He hooked a thumb toward the young man. "This is Buddy Jenkins, my new assistant."

Mutzi studied the guy. Twenty, maybe older. Hard to tell. A little rough around the edges, but apparently not afraid to get his hands dirty. "Did Chuck tell you we're trips?" She loved watching people's reactions whenever she told them.

Buddy looked at Chuck, confusion written all over his scrunched face. "What's that mean?"

"Marge, Mutzi, and I are triplets."

"Wow. That's cool. Bet it was fun growing up together."

This part always got a little complicated, but Mutzi never tired of telling it in her own creative way. "Marge and I grew up thinking we were twins. Imagine finding out on our sixty-fifth birthday we had a brother. The doc decided three kids were too many for one woman to raise, so he gave away the trouble-maker"—she tipped her head toward her brother—"to another woman."

She laughed and winked at Chuck. "Now we're one big happy family. Well, most of the time, anyway."

Chuck nodded. "Mutzi's the real trouble-maker in the family. Watch out for her." He looked at Buddy. "Can you handle the rest of the wood? I want to go inside and fill Mutzi in on some things."

"Yes, sir." He turned and left.

"Since when do you get an assistant and we don't?" she teased.

Chuck held the door open for her. "Since I do all the heavy lifting." He grew serious. "The man was living on the street. Thought he needed a break. He's a good worker. Just needs a little guidance."

"You'll be a great mentor, though I'll deny I ever said that if you tell anyone."

Chuck mussed her hair. "Such a hard a…"

Mutzi giggled, knowing what he intended to say, but with Marge within earshot, he dared not curse.

"Hi." Marge had sorted out all of the pantry items and had them distributed all over the kitchen in an orderly fashion.

Wide-eyed, Mutzi laughed. "Looks like the pantry exploded. What's going on?"

Chuck glanced at Marge and winked. "I didn't like the way she's arranged everything, so I told her to start over."

Marge's face reddened. "You did not."

He laughed. "A communication snafu. I asked Buddy to paint a shelf. He decided all the shelves needed a fresh coat, so he emptied everything—into one big heap."

A smile lit Marge's face. "Actually, I'm glad he did it. It looks clean and fresh, and I thought of a better way to organize my pots and pans. Things happen for a reason. I just didn't have it on my schedule for today."

"That schedule's been pretty full lately. Thought I'd come by and give you a hand after we're done here, if you'd like." Mutzi wrinkled her nose. "Are your cookies burning?"

Marge gasped, then grabbed two mitts and rushed to the oven. "Darn it. There goes another batch."

Chuck peered over her shoulder. "How many batches have you scorched this week?"

She elbowed him to move aside.

Mutzi looked at Chuck. "Martha Stewart's clone burned something? Impossible. What's this world coming to?"

Tossing the oven mitts on top of the stack of metal pans, Marge tore off her apron and snipped at Mutzi, "You've charred enough meals for both of us. Guess it was my turn."

The memory of almost burning down Marge's house never faded from Mutzi's mind even though it had been many years ago. She didn't need the cruel reminder. The snide remark seemed out of place, but Marge had been under a lot of stress lately. "Hey, don't get your panties in a wad. I was joking. I burned eggs this morning. Stuff happens."

Mutzi followed Marge into the great room.

Chuck joined them. "What's going on?"

Tears brimmed Marge's eyes but didn't spill.

"Nothing. I over-baked a batch or two of cookies." She turned away from them. "I'll stop at the store and buy some for the woman's club meeting tomorrow."

Mutzi offered, "I can do that. You don't have to do everything yourself."

"You'd probably embarrass me by bringing those little animal cookies you love so much."

The words stung. It wasn't like Marge to sling insults, but she was doing a fine job of it today. Mutzi had enough. "Have it your way, Ms. Perfect." She turned to leave. "I'll do you one better. I won't come to the meeting, that way you won't be humiliated by me."

Just as Mutzi reached the front door, she heard a loud thump and turned around.

"Marge!" Chuck shouted as he knelt by her side and checked for a pulse. "Mutzi! Get a cold cloth from the bathroom."

The circle of crows had warned her yesterday. *Not Marge. Not now. Not after what I said to her.* The words pressed on her chest like a leaded blanket.

"Mutzi! Hurry! A cold cloth!"

Frozen in place, she didn't move. Couldn't move.

"Mutzi." Chuck's voice faded.

She no longer heard him, only her own voice. "I killed my sister."

Chapter Ten

Chuck's face was inches from Mutzi when she opened her eyes, standing in the same place near the front door. Chuck's hands gently grasped her shoulders. *Where am I? What happened? Focus.*

He pointed across the room. "Marge is okay, Mutzi. Look."

Her sister offered a little wave from the couch. "I'm alive, Sis. I just fainted."

It took a few moments for the words to filter through Mutzi's muddled brain. How long had she been out? Mentally checking out hadn't happened to her for many years. She knew the medical term but couldn't remember it. She closed her eyes and tried to concentrate.

"Mutzi." Chuck's voice called, firmer this time.

She opened her eyes again. Chuck, Buddy, and Shadow stood within an arm's length watching her.

Marge patted the sofa. "Come, sit down next to me." She moved a pillow to make room.

Chuck touched her arm and led her to the couch. The frightening scene replayed in her mind. Harsh words. A loud thump. Her sister flat on the floor.

Marge gazed up at Mutzi, her eyes filled with regret. "I'm so sorry. I was rude. I don't know what got into me."

Mutzi settled on the plush sofa. "You scared the hell out of me—and don't expect me to apologize for cursing. I thought you were dead."

"Good news. I'm not." Marge offered a weak smile. "Are you feeling better?"

More clear-headed now, Mutzi nodded. "Yeah. I freaked out. Couldn't even help when you needed me."

"The men took good care of us." Marge met Buddy's eyes. "Chuck was right. We do need you around here."

A smile spread across Buddy's face.

The young man knelt in front of Mutzi and spoke. "Your mind shut down to protect you because you were scared. When something real bad happens, sometimes our mind checks out." He added, "It's called dissociation—fight, flight, or freeze. I tend to take off—flight. I guess you freeze."

She recognized the word. "Right. That's what it's called." The simple explanation was spot on. It wasn't the first time Mutzi had experienced it and probably wouldn't be the last. Apparently, she and Buddy had something in common. "Sounds like you've been through it, too. We'll have to talk about it later."

"I'd like that. Not many people understand what's going on inside you when it happens. I used to do it a lot, but it's better now."

Chuck rubbed his hands together. "You ladies sit here and rest while Buddy and I fix some tea."

A blast of chilly air traveled through the room just as the men retreated into the kitchen drawing Mutzi's attention to the open front door.

Rose Ellen had arrived unnoticed. She grunted as she struggled to drag two overstuffed bags through the door. "No one could come carry these bags, but you've got time for a tea party?"

Her oldest sister had a poor sense of timing. Mutzi sighed. "Late as usual."

Marge pressed a hand on the arm of the couch, attempting to get up. Mutzi reached out and urged her to stay seated. "Don't. Let Rose Ellen take care of herself...for a change."

Rose Ellen huffed as she dropped the bags and plopped in a chair. "Well, I guess I know where I stand."

"What is all that?" Marge asked.

With an exaggerated sigh, Rose Ellen responded. "Well, while you ladies were sitting around sipping tea, I was busy gathering some finishing touches for this place."

Mutzi exchanged a wary glance with Marge who again tried to get up. She settled back on the couch and closed her eyes. "Still light-headed?"

Marge nodded, then looked at Rose Ellen. "What finishing touches?"

"You'll see." Rose Ellen wagged a finger in Marge's direction. "You need to watch getting up so fast. You're getting older you know."

The words ignited a flame in Mutzi this time. "While you were out shopping, your sister was flat on the floor—half dead."

Rose Ellen rolled her eyes. "You do love to exaggerate. What are you talking about?"

Marge dismissed the concern with a flip of her hand. "It's nothing. Go on with what you were saying."

"Well, you can relax now. I'm here to help get this place into shape."

Marge's face turned beet red. "What do you think I've been doing for months?" Her voice rose an octave. "This place is exactly as we want it. You fly in here at the last minute and think you can change everything to fit your style. That's not going to happen, no matter how much money you dangle in front of us."

"Calm down, Sis." Mutzi feared her sister might pass out again.

Chuck returned carrying a tray. "What's going on?"

Both sisters glared at Rose Ellen, waiting for her to explain.

She rolled her eyes, then turned to Chuck. "You and I agreed—"

He set the tray down and threw a hand up. "Stop right there. We did not agree on anything. Actually, we disagreed on some things and then you high-tailed it out of here when I said we'd discuss any changes with Marge."

Rose Ellen stood and grabbed her bags. "If you're all going to fight with me, I'll take my money and leave. Then what will you do about your leaky roof?"

The corner of Chuck's lip curled. "It was nice of you to offer to help, but the roof is fixed and it didn't cost a dime. We're not going to need your money—at least not now." He took the bags from her and said, "I can take these to your car, or we can all sit down and discuss whatever it is you want to discuss." He waited for a response. "Which will it be?"

Rose Ellen looked at her sisters and then back to Chuck. "I'd like to stay, if it's all right with everyone."

Marge and Chuck nodded. Mutzi remained uncommitted. She didn't want to widen the divide between them, but it wouldn't hurt her feelings if her oldest sister bowed out.

Rose Ellen eased back into the chair. Chuck set the bags down and distributed the tea. They drank in silence. When the cups were empty, Mutzi placed them on the tray and headed to the kitchen. Buddy was busy putting the pots and pans back in the pantry.

"You should wait for Marge to tell you where to put everything. She has a plan, I'm sure." She nudged his arm. "You might as well be part of the family fun. Come on. Let's go back in and listen."

When they walked into the great room, Rose Ellen stopped talking and looked at Buddy. "Who's he?"

"Buddy, this is our old...er sister, Rose Ellen." Mutzi snickered. The introduction appeared to be sufficient and the jab ignored.

"Here's what I was thinking," she began. "It would be good if we had one room designed for guests who like a little more luxury." She leaned forward toward Marge. "You did a lovely job with everything. The bedroom I looked at fits perfectly with the rustic charm of this place."

"Then what is there to change?" Marge folded her arms.

"I heard through the grapevine that Sylvia Montgomery is one of your first guests. I happen to know she is an influencer—a philanthropist who donates six figures annually to numerous causes. Someone like that could mean success or failure for our business."

"Go on." Marge leaned back.

"I thought if you had one room designed with a little more luxury, it might be beneficial." Rose Ellen opened one of the bags and revealed a magnificent bedspread with a jacquard-woven design. She handed it to Marge. "I have matching curtains." She opened the other bag enough for them to see. "I thought the champagne, eggplant, and dark blue colors would complement the floors and furniture."

Marge seemed to be weighing all the information before responding. "They are beautiful and you're right, they would add a nice touch to the room." She stroked the soft linen. "I understand your reasoning. I'm not sure I understand the need to impress Ms. Montgomery, but if Mutzi and Chuck agree, I'm willing to make changes to one bedroom."

"Sounds good to me," Chuck said. "How about you, Mutzi?"

"Anything to keep peace in the family." She added, "Provided you don't have any more surprises up your sleeve." She studied Rose Ellen's face and noticed her mouth twitch, a sure sign she'd planned more. From the look on Marge's face, she'd noticed it, too.

"Is that all?" Marge asked.

As if Rose Ellen had been prodded with a poker, she jumped up. "I better head back before it gets dark." Picking up her purse, she paused and asked Marge, "You'll take care of the bedroom issue, then?"

"The issue? If you mean change the linens—yes. In *one* room." She massaged her neck. "Be safe driving home."

Once Rose Ellen left, Mutzi vented. "Bet she ordered a bunch more things she had to cancel. She's a piece of work, that one."

Chuck added, "She did mention something about leather furniture. You don't think she would have ordered that without talking to us, do you?"

"Apparently, you don't know Rose Ellen. If she wanted it, she wouldn't wait to get a consensus."

Chuck dipped his head and sighed. "What an afternoon." He walked to Buddy and placed a hand on his shoulder. "Welcome to the family drama. Let's go check on that paint. It should be dry."

"It is. I started putting things back"—his eyes grew wide as he directed his attention to Marge—"but, Mutzi said you'd prefer to tell me where you want everything, so I stopped."

Marge smiled. "Let's do it together. I'll make another batch of cookies while you fill the shelves. Deal?"

"Yes, ma'am!"

Chapter Eleven

T he grandfather clock in Marge's hallway bonged eleven times. Mutzi had followed her home and gone to bed an hour earlier. Satisfied there was nothing else to accomplish tonight, Marge turned off the kitchen light and walked into the foyer just as Ashley, her college boarder and soon to be co-manager of the lodge, slipped a key into the door lock.

The petite strawberry blonde smiled when she saw Marge. "My last late night. Promise." She dropped her backpack on the table. "You look exhausted. Rough day?" She moved closer. "Need to talk about it?"

There was a time when Marge would have hesitated sharing her burdens with anyone, much less a twenty-two-year-old. She'd come to appreciate Ashley's often logical and supportive thoughts. "Let's see. I burnt two batches of cookies, yelled at Mutzi, passed out, and fought with Rose Ellen. That about sums it up."

"Oh, my. That is a tough day."

"I'll be all right. I just need to get a grip on prioritizing my commitments. I let things get out of hand."

Ashley reached for Marge's hand. "I don't think prioritizing is going to fix your problem. You're trying to fill the emptiness in your heart with motion. All your commitments are just movement. It's like sitting in a rocking chair and expecting to get somewhere."

"Okay, my wise friend." Marge tipped her head. "What do you propose I do instead?"

She squeezed Marge's hand a little tighter. "Love someone." With a glint in her eyes, she added, "You need to love and to be loved."

Marge chuckled and turned her head to break the eye contact. "I love many people, and they love me." Ashley's frown didn't go unnoticed. "You think I need a man?"

"Yes. In your case, a man." A slow nod affirmed the words. "Rumi once wrote, *There is a candle in your heart, ready to be kindled. There is a void in your soul, ready to be filled. You feel it, don't you?*" Ashley paused long enough to let Marge consider the quote. "You can continue to fill every day with commitments or you can open your heart to other opportunities. Your choice."

Ashley released Marge's hand and walked toward her room. "Think about it."

"I will. Good night."

"'Night."

As Marge lay in bed with her eyes closed, Ashley's advice replayed in her mind. Somewhere between the comfort of the bedsheets and the luminous morning sun shimmering through the wooden blinds, clarity and inspiration formed a new awareness. She stepped into the shower with a joyful tune playing in her head.

The earthy, rich scent of coffee drew her to the kitchen. "Morning."

The unexpected greeting startled Marge. She'd forgotten Mutzi had spent the night. "Good morning."

Her sister poured a cup of coffee and set it on the counter. "So, what can I help you with today?"

Picking up the steamy mug, Marge closed her eyes and savored a hint of vanilla in the smooth, warm liquid. Just yesterday, she'd resisted her sister's offer for help. Today, she welcomed it with a new mindset. "We need to fill the baskets for the guest rooms at the lodge. There are three bags in the hall closet. But, let's have a little breakfast first. What shall I make?"

Mutzi shook her head. "Nothing. Let's keep it simple. Bagels and cream cheese?"

The suggestion brought a smile to Marge's face. "Sounds good to me. One less thing to do. There's a bowl of fruit cocktail in the fridge."

The two worked together, setting the table and gathering the food.

"Just like old times. I've missed this." Marge smiled as she nibbled on a cinnamon raisin bagel.

Mutzi popped a grape in her mouth and nodded. "We had it down to a smooth rhythm, didn't we?"

"Being alone in this house took some getting used to after you moved in with Sam." Marge glanced around. The large Victorian was more than she needed. Would she be able to co-manage the lodge and keep up with maintaining this place? Doubt lingered, then she brushed it away.

"I know what you mean. Sam's never home anymore. And I hate being there all by myself. Well, I do have Midnight, but he doesn't talk much. It's easy to slip into bad habits without Sam around."

"Bad habits? Is there something I should be concerned about?"

"Nope. You've got enough to handle without my silliness."

The two sisters finished eating in silence, each lost in her own thoughts. Marge carried her cup to the sink. She smiled to herself knowing *this* sister would do the same without prompting. "Shall we get started?"

"Yep. I'll get the bags." Mutzi added her mug to the dishwasher and headed down the hall. She returned with the goodies, peeking in the sacks to see what they held.

In the dining room, Marge placed eight hand-woven baskets on the table. They'd be filled with a wide assortment of items meant to encourage peace and relaxation. While the lodge would host only six guests this first time, she decided Chuck and Buddy could benefit from the hodge-podge of tools, too.

From one of the bags, Marge removed liners she'd sewn and tucked them into the belly of each basket.

"Where did you find time to make all these?" Mutzi lifted the last one and admired the paisley print of the material. "They're absolutely beautiful, as usual. You're amazing."

Beaming, Marge added, "I made these, too." She held up a few three-by-three-inch swatches of plush cloth with stitching sewn in unique patterns. "I got the idea online. They call them silent fidgets. Rubbing them—like a worry stone—releases stress for some people."

"Brilliant." Mutzi massaged it between her thumb and finger. "I can see where these would be soothing. Great idea." Next, she took out an assortment of pens and journals. "These are cool, too."

"I think it's really important for guests to write about their concerns and experiences." Marge added one of each to a container. "It's funny how you start seeing problems in a different light once you reread what you've recorded." It had been a while since Marge had written her thoughts. Perhaps she'd keep one for herself and start writing again.

Mutzi squeezed a rubbery stress ball and tossed it at Marge, laughing when it bounced off her shoulder and landed on the floor.

"You can pick that up." Marge grinned. "Always the playful child." She handed Mutzi a few more items to distribute. "We probably need to talk about what we'll do to keep the guests entertained once they arrive."

"I've been thinking about that. I found a nature hike, which might help them reconnect with earthly matters. You know, looking for spiderwebs early in the morning when the dew is still clinging to them. We can encourage them to appreciate God's creations, since they probably don't make time during their hectic days to do that."

Marge added, "How about a garden area where they can plant something? Working with dirt can be therapeutic and gives the mind time to rewind. What else?"

"Bonfires at night, with s'mores of course. Star gazing provides perspective. It has a way of making troubles seem less significant."

"We'll need something indoors in case of bad weather."

Mutzi's eyes lit up. "Thankful pumpkins. I've got a dozen black markers, the kind with fine tips. Every day, guests write something on the pumpkin they're grateful for. The goal will be to fill the entire pumpkin by the time their week is up."

"I love that idea. We can make our own and use them for decorations." Marge arranged the items in each basket until she was pleased with the finished product. "We will also have music, meditation tapes, books, and group discussions."

"I have another idea. I'll take a picture of each guest, print it on cardboard, and make them into puzzles. Each time they discover something about themselves, we'll give them a piece of their puzzle. Connecting the pieces of their life."

Marge considered the idea. "That could work if there weren't too many pieces." She stared at Mutzi. "You come up with the most original ideas. I'm glad you've been a part of this."

"Wonder if Rose Ellen learned anything yesterday. I know I did."

"Hopefully." Marge paused, realizing she'd learned quite a few things herself. For one, too much stress can make you faint. "What did you learn, Sis?"

She looked up. "The power of words."

The simple summation struck home with Marge. Her sharp words had started the squabble that had preceded her fainting spell and Mutzi's dissociation. "Very true." She crossed the room and gave her sister a hug. "I'm so sorry for yesterday."

"Wasn't all your fault. I shouldn't have teased you about burning the cookies."

Marge glanced at the clock. "Guess we better finish up and get to the meeting. We have a lot of business items on the Woman's Club agenda today."

"I almost forgot. Sam and I are meeting for dinner at Montaluce afterwards. We were supposed to last night, but since we got delayed at the lodge, we rescheduled for tonight. Want to join us?"

"That's sweet of you to offer, but you should spend some quiet time with Sam. I know you haven't had much of that lately."

"You're right. It's been hard." She released a deep sigh. "I don't know how you do it living in this big old house all by yourself."

"Ashley's still here, but she is gone most of the time. I stay busy. That's how I get overwhelmed with too many commitments. I've been trying to fill the void."

"You need a man."

Marge stared at her sister. "That's what Ashley suggested last night." She shook her head. "It's not like I don't have enough to do already. Besides, I don't see any men lining up at my door." She picked up her purse and handed the cookie tin to Mutzi. "I was blessed to have George. Having a man like him only happens once in your life."

Lifting the lid on the tin, Mutzi snitched a cookie. "You never know what life has in store." She nibbled an oatmeal chocolate chip Marge had baked to perfection. "Mmm, good. You haven't lost your touch."

Chapter Twelve

T he Dahlonega Woman's Club finished on schedule, leaving Mutzi with an extra hour before meeting Sam for dinner. The church parking lot was empty except for one car. She parked next to it and then traipsed inside.

Mutzi peeked into Reverend Mitch's office. Only the top of her pastor's head was visible above the mounds of books and paper on his desk. She considered knocking, but the playful side of her skipped the announcement. Stepping into the room, she asked, "Still shuffling papers?"

The startled man's hand jerked, tipping over the half-empty cup of coffee sitting to his right. Papers flew everywhere.

Mutzi grabbed some tissues and helped sop it up. "Sorry." She hadn't planned on creating a catastrophe, but she enjoyed getting a rise out of the normally calm, cool preacher. "I thought you were going to get a computer."

"Oh, I got the computer." He pointed to a box in the corner of the room. "But it doesn't come with a book of instructions—or an extra set of hands."

A twinge of guilt tugged at her conscience. The weekly bulletin had sought someone to fill a volunteer position in the office for months. So far, the request had gone unanswered, but not unseen. Mutzi looked beyond the messy desk to stacks of documents piled on top of two chairs, the credenza, and even some boxes in the corner of the room.

She drew in a deep breath and released it through pursed lips. "So, here's the deal. I'll get your computer set up, organize"—her hand swept wide—"all this, and teach you how to work electronically." She paused and then added, "But you have to do something for me."

Her offer brought a chuckle from Reverend Mitch. "You are something else, Mutzi McGilvray Parks." He shook his head. "Quid pro quo?" He rubbed his face and glanced around the room. "Is it legal?" A belly laugh followed his question.

She folded her arms against her chest, slightly annoyed and yet humored at the question. "Come on. You know me better than that. I've been confessing my sins to you as long as I can remember."

His smile disappeared. "True. What's on your mind?"

"This deacon training. It's been tough, for Sam, and for me. I know he's called to do it, but it sure has been lonesome without him."

"I'm sure it hasn't been easy. There's a reason deacons, like priests, normally aren't married. Choosing to devote your life to the church is a serious commitment. I can't change the process, if that's what you're wanting."

"No. I have to suck it up—oh, crap—" She gnawed on a nail. "I'm sorry for cursing. Do I need to include those in my confession on Saturday, or does this qualify?"

Reverend Mitch's mouth twitched with a suppressed grin. "Just continue."

"Sam's going to be ordained soon. I know the archbishop makes the final decision where to place him, but as the pastor, you have influence. Right?"

Reverend Mitch drew in a deep breath and released a slow sigh. "It's a complicated matter, Mutzi. There's a major shortage of clergy in the church, and we already have one deacon assigned to this location."

"You're saying this won't be his designated parish? That's not fair. This is where he belongs."

"I agree. But that's not how it works, my friend. Pastors don't get to make the decision. There are other locations in Georgia in desperate need."

"We are *not* moving!" The thought infuriated Mutzi. Sam loved their acreage as much as she did. The only alternative option was for him to drive back and forth from who knows where. The thought of spending more hours in the empty house sent her over the edge. Before she could say anything more she might regret, Mutzi spun on her heels and stormed out.

Chapter Thirteen

With the morning rush hour traffic behind her, Rose Ellen pressed on the gas pedal, hoping to time her arrival at the lodge just right. Chuck and Marge both had business in town again. She hadn't exactly been truthful when they asked what else she'd wanted to change when it came to the lodge decor. Based on their reactions to her suggestions, they'd be furious with her purchases.

The furniture company had agreed to cancel the order she'd placed for the new leather couch and chairs. Unfortunately, the in-stock tables and lamps were already on the way to the lodge. With any luck, she'd be there in time to refuse the delivery, and her siblings would never know she'd ordered them without their approval.

Seeing the empty parking spaces near the lodge brought a sigh of relief. Perhaps she'd made it in time. Rose Ellen parked and hurried to the front door expecting to find the key in the same location as before. It wasn't there. She lifted the welcome mat and looked under it.

Suddenly, the door swung open.

"Did you lose something?"

The unexpected voice and figure in the doorway startled Rose Ellen. She stifled a scream. "You scared the daylights out of me. Who are you?"

"Buddy." He held the door open. "We met the other day."

"We did?" She stopped and stared at him, trying to remember his face.

"The day Marge fainted and Mutzi checked out."

Even more confused, Rose Ellen strained to envision the chaotic scene. "Whatever are you talking about? When did Marge faint?" She'd only been at the lodge a couple of times. Surely, she'd remember that!

Buddy stared as if he wasn't sure what else to say.

"Was I here when that happened?" Her voice rose in disbelief.

"No. You came in right after."

A wave of nausea washed over her. *Why was all this so unfamiliar?* "Tell me what happened."

"Well," Buddy said and shoved his hands in his pockets. "Marge got upset with me for messing up her pantry and then she burnt a batch of cookies, which made her more unhappy. Then, she and Mutzi argued, and Marge fainted." He shrugged and then continued. "Mutzi thought Marge had died and she zoned out."

"How could I have forgotten something like that?" Her pulse pounded in her ears and she wiped perspiration from her forehead. Perhaps her sisters didn't tell her. That must be it. "I came in after all this happened?"

Buddy nodded.

Somewhat reassured she wasn't losing her memory, Rose Ellen set her purse on the foyer table and removed her luxurious pashmina. When she looked around the great room, her mouth dropped open. "Oh, no." The sleek steel end tables sat next to the classic lodge sofa. The modern black and white lamps clashed with the rustic wood throughout the room. "What have I done?" She muttered to herself.

Rose Ellen eased into one of the chairs and fanned herself with one hand. "Where's the furniture that was here before?"

"I put it out in the shed." He glanced around the room and shrugged. "I don't think this goes together."

"You are so right." She stood and unplugged a lamp, cradling it in her arm. "Will you help me switch everything back to the way it was—before anyone else notices it?"

Buddy grabbed one of the tables and followed her.

Sweat trickled down Rose Ellen's neck by the time they finished. Exhausted, she plopped down on the couch and picked up one of the throw pillows and hugged it to her chest. The plush material soothed her as she stroked it. "This isn't bad. It's actually pretty comfy." *Perhaps others will like it too.*

Another thought struck her. "What am I going to do with the stuff we took to the shed?"

Buddy paused and then offered, "I can sell it for you."

Rose Ellen sat up and leaned forward. "How would you do that without Chuck knowing? This needs to be our little secret." She put a finger to her lip and shook her head. "No. Don't tell me. It's probably better I don't know."

"Okay." Buddy stared out the window and the color drained from his face. "I gotta go. Tell him you've never heard of me." He turned and raced out the back door.

She looked outside and saw a patrol car parked next to hers. A uniformed officer got out. Meeting him at the door, she asked, "What's going on?"

"Looking for Chuck Hansen. Is he here?"

"No. What do you want with him?"

"That's none of your business. Do you know when he'll be back?"

"No. I don't." Her mind spun, trying to imagine why the law would be looking for Chuck. Did it have something to do with the lodge, or could Buddy be in some kind of trouble?

The officer started to move past her. "Mind if I look around?"

Her gut and sixth sense screamed trouble. "I do mind." They locked eyes and she didn't blink. "You need to leave. Now."

The young officer stood a few inches over Rose Ellen. He drew his brows tight and pursed his lips. "Rest assured. I *will* be back."

Unintimidated by his threat, Rose Ellen stretched tall. "You better have a warrant." She didn't know why she'd said that, but she hoped it would keep him from snooping around until she knew what he was up to. When the patrol car drove away, she called out for Buddy without getting a response. *He must have hidden in the woods.* No way she was going out there to find him.

The strange morning wore on her mind. Buddy's sudden disappearance. His story about Marge's and Mutzi's dramatic experiences. The early arrival of the delivery truck and the unfortunate selection of furniture. What else could go wrong? She shook her head and reprimanded herself out loud. "I know better than to ever ask that!"

She picked up her purse and shawl to leave before Chuck returned. Her cell phone played *April in Paris*, the tone programmed for her daughter, as she headed to the car.

"Hi, honey," Rose Ellen said nonchalantly. "Is everything okay?"

Chapter Fourteen

The following morning, Chuck glanced at the clock and shook his head, surprised and disappointed he'd overslept. He'd wanted to get more brush cut outside. Instead, he'd only had enough time for a shower and shave. Wandering through the lodge, he called for Buddy. Other than the radio blaring, there was no answer. He walked outside and looked around.

Shadow roamed around the empty parking space. It took a moment to register. "Where the hell's my truck?" The words echoed through the nearby woods. Anger rose through his body and settled into his chest with a sharp stab. Had Buddy stolen his truck?

How could he have been so foolish, so gullible? What would he do without wheels? It had taken him weeks to get on the city planner's schedule. The lodge wouldn't open on time without the final permits.

Digging his cell phone from his pocket, he contemplated who to call first: The City Planner's Office? Marge? The police? His fingers froze as he weighed his decision. A hint of hope edged its way forward. Maybe the transient would come back in time.

His mind struggled to sort out the right thing to do. Would Buddy really steal his truck? He'd been respectful, a hard worker. *But what do I really know about him other than he was homeless?*

Trusting his instincts, Chuck dialed the one person with nearly as much at stake as him. "Hi, Sandi." He didn't waste time with chitchat. "I've got truck issues and can't make the meeting for the permits. Can you fill in? It's at ten thirty."

A brief pause, then she spoke. "I'll have to rearrange my schedule, but I'll be there. You're going to owe me big time."

He wasn't sure what that would entail, but he was in no place to argue. "I understand, but remember I do have my limits," he teased.

"With the traffic in Atlanta, I need to leave now. Talk to you later." The call ended.

As he walked back inside, the end of a news story on the radio involving the Crisson Gold Mine made him cringe. It had been more than a year since the collapse at the Consolidated Gold Mine, yet the memory of that day when he landed in jail accused of robbery and sexual assault still haunted him. At least he couldn't be accused of being involved in this fiasco, whatever it was.

Diverting the painful memory to the back of his mind, Chuck focused on how to handle his current situation—Buddy and the missing truck. The guy had been infatuated with the vehicle and had asked several times if he could drive it. Chuck had held back giving him permission, but had never really said no. Of all the days to test his limits. Not today when so much was riding on this last meeting.

The grueling process of opening the lodge had taken its toll on all of them. Marge, stressed out with too many commitments, had passed out. Apparently, Mutzi had some issues he wasn't aware of as well. Now this. Would the three of them be able to run the Skipping Stone Lodge? The siblings were all at an age where most people retire, yet here they were trying to start a business. Doubt continued its threat to overwhelm him.

He took a deep breath and released it with precision. Be patient, his heart told him. His mind battled with the possibility of never seeing Buddy or the truck again. He could have wrecked it or sold it to someone for all he knew. He didn't even know if Buddy had a license. Would his impulsive decision to help the homeless guy come back to haunt him?

Chuck rubbed the gripping pain in his chest. He'd always prided himself with being able to tell the good guys from the bad. Buddy displayed potential. He worked hard, showed respect, and listened. Surely those were good traits and not a cover for someone with bad intentions. Angst and faith continued to seesaw within him.

The familiar hum of tires on the blacktop road urged Chuck back outside. He squinted, trying to get a closer look through the thick woods. Definitely a truck, same color as his. Hope edged ahead of doubt as the vehicle turned onto the gravel road leading to the lodge. The tightness in his chest eased a fraction with relief.

Chuck hurried to the parking space as Buddy pulled up. The moment the engine quieted, Chuck whipped open the driver's door. "Where the hell have you been? Do you know how much trouble you're in? I almost had you arrested for stealing my truck. You knew I had an important meeting this morning. What were you thinking?"

Buddy eased out, handed the keys to Chuck, and backed away. Fear drained the color from his young face. "I'm sorry, mister." He trembled near the bed of the truck.

Shame at his outburst diffused Chuck's bitterness. "You can't just take off and not expect me to be upset."

The boy shook his head. "I would never steal from you."

"You did exactly that. When you take something that's not yours, you're stealing."

Buddy's eyes brimmed with moisture. "You said we needed more mulch, but you were too busy to get it."

Chuck raised his eyes to the sky, searching his mind for a hint of the conversation, and then remembered. "And you offered to go this morning." He rubbed his forehead, wishing he'd remembered the conversation sooner.

Buddy responded with a nod. "I was just borrowing the truck, with your permission."

"Crap. I'm sorry." Chuck's shoulders dropped and he hung his head. "I screwed up. I've got so much on my mind. I freaked out when I couldn't find you." The horrible accusations he'd flung at this young man made his stomach turn. "I'm so sorry. I'm so very sorry."

Buddy moved closer, gave Chuck a brief hug, then stepped back.

The unexpected action caused Chuck to stammer. "Wha...what's that for?"

"For not giving me a beating." He smiled and added, "And especially for saying you're sorry. No one's ever said that to me before."

The words revealed the young man's life story. Chuck returned the hug and patted Buddy's head. "There's no shame in admitting your mistakes. I'll always own up to my own actions, and I want you to do the same."

Buddy's face brightened. "I'll get the mulch unloaded right away. You've still got time to make the meeting."

Chuck glanced at his watch. "I'll give you a hand."

Buddy lowered the tailgate and the two worked in silence as they piled the heavy bags next to the truck.

With the last one stacked, Chuck withdrew a handkerchief and wiped his hands. "You know where I want them spread, right?"

"Yes, sir. I'll take care of it while you're gone to town."

Chuck hurried inside, grabbed a folder, and returned to his truck. Buddy disappeared around the back of the lodge with a bag of mulch balanced on each shoulder. As Chuck drove away, he offered a prayer of thanks for Buddy's safe return and another for being able to recognize a good guy when he saw one.

Chapter Fifteen

T he phone vibrated in Chuck's pocket as he waited in the City Planner's office for the board to give their final approval. He slipped it out from his jeans and glanced at the screen, intending only to check who sent the text. Stroking his freshly shaved chin, he frowned. *Rose Ellen?*

Curious, he continued to read. *"An officer came looking for you at the lodge yesterday. He wouldn't say what he wanted, but asked to snoop around. I told him no. Buddy took off when he saw the patrol car."* The message jolted him. Why would the police want to talk to him? He hadn't had so much as a parking ticket since his release from jail. He read the text again. Why was Rose Ellen at the lodge and why would Buddy run off?

Chuck felt Sandi's eyes on him even before she spoke.

"What's going on?" Her black ponytail fell over her shoulder when she tilted her head.

He shrugged. "Nothing."

"Bull. Your boot is tapping a hole in the floor."

Chuck pressed a hand on his knee, forcing his foot to stop jittering. "I got a text from Rose Ellen."

She folded her arms and sighed. "You know I'm going to hound you until you tell me what's going on."

True. The woman would have no mercy on him. She could break down all his defenses. It had been a blessing and a curse. "Rose Ellen was at the lodge yesterday."

"Why? I thought you and Marge tempered her interest in changing things."

Chuck ran a hand through his hair. "I don't know why." He released a puff of air before passing the phone to her.

Sandi read the text. When she finished, her deep brown eyes drilled through Chuck as if searching for more information. If he'd been hiding anything, she'd have known. He'd have spilled his guts. *Damn. She'd make a great interrogator.*

"Do you know what this is about?"

Chuck shook his head. "I have no clue why the cops would be looking for me. I'm surprised Rose Ellen told the officer no when he asked to look around."

"She's a smart woman." Sandi handed the phone back. "Buddy's the guy you told me about, right? Why would he run off?"

It embarrassed him to say the answer out loud. "I have no idea." Why hadn't he asked Buddy more questions?

Had his decision to offer the young man refuge been a mistake? He knew so little about him. Was he running from the law? What if Chuck was harboring a fugitive? He'd been foolish to rely solely on his instincts.

Chuck leaned forward and buried his head in his hands, exhausted from the stress. It had been one thing after another. He'd been unprepared for the grueling process of opening the lodge. The reason the place set empty for so many years became clearer each step of the way. He'd underestimated the time, patience, and money needed to complete all the necessary work. Offering refuge to Buddy was supposed to be a good thing. Now, he wasn't so sure. Fear of having made another wrong decision weighed heavily. There was so much at stake—not just him, but for Sandi, Marge, and Mutzi, too.

Sandi reached over and touched his arm. "Don't start worrying about things that haven't happened. You've managed to get through every crisis. The goal post is right in front of you. It's all going to work out fine. Trust me. Trust yourself."

His gut churned despite her encouragement. He lifted his head and looked away from her. "I'm trying."

The office door opened, and the city planner stepped through it. Chuck stood on shaky legs. Sandi joined him.

"The board signed off on everything. Providing the food service inspection passes, you're cleared to open. We'll send someone out to post the permits on Tuesday.

Chuck turned to Sandi, wrapped her in a bear hug, and lifted her off the floor. He wanted to kiss her ruby red lips, but restrained himself, respecting the ground rules established when they became partners. Instead, he directed a soft peck to her cheek and released his hold on her. "We did it." He couldn't wipe the grin from his face.

"You did it. You did all the planning, heavy lifting, and worrying." She picked up her purse and slipped the strap over her shoulder. "Dreams can become reality. You need to believe in yourself, Chuck."

The watch on his arm buzzed, interrupting the sweet moment. "I need to get back. The food inspector's going to be at the lodge within an hour. I have to run, but let's celebrate with dinner tonight."

She shook her head. "Sorry. I've got plans."

Air seeped from his briefly inflated bubble. "Oh, okay. No problem." He wanted more from their relationship, but it seemed the feelings weren't mutual.

"I'll see you Sunday." She leaned close and whispered in his ear. "You still owe me."

The emotional bubble reinflated a bit as they walked out. This was one debt he looked forward to paying.

Chapter Sixteen

The white panel truck arrived two hours earlier than scheduled, but this time Marge had anticipated it. She'd baked zucchini bread at the crack of dawn, so the stove would have time to cool. The kitchen counters, cabinets, floor, and every utensil shined to perfection. She and Chuck had checked each item on the pre-inspection list to make sure nothing could go wrong.

Marge watched Leroy from the window as he strapped on his work belt and grabbed his clipboard. When he reached the back door, he knocked instead of barging in like the first day. Marge couldn't help but smile.

"Food Service Inspector," he announced.

She pulled the door open. "Good morning, Leroy. Come in."

The corner of his lip rose just enough for Marge to glimpse it, then it was gone. Professional Inspector returned.

He sniffed the air and frowned. "Did you bake again? You know I can't inspect that oven unless it's cool."

She walked to the stove, opened the oven door, and put her hand on the metal rack. "Cool as a cucumber."

Without responding, he moved toward the walk-in freezer and opened it. He ran his hand down the new magnetic stripping, nodded, and made a note.

Marge slipped off her apron and hung it on a hook. "I'll be in the other room. Please let me know when you've finished." She wandered into the dining hall, removed a stack of napkins from the credenza, and refolded them, trying to busy herself while Leroy, still silent as a church mouse in the kitchen, continued with the inspection.

Twenty minutes later, he found her and cleared his throat. "I'm done."

Marge nodded and walked into the kitchen.

"Everything's in order. You've passed inspection." He glanced up from his paperwork. "Please remember to wear a hairnet and gloves when serving."

"Thank you. I won't forget." She slipped her apron over her head and tied it. "Now that my offer can't be considered a bribe, would you like a cup of coffee and some zucchini bread?"

He smirked. "Guess I deserve that...but I was just doing my job." He pulled a stool from under the island and sat.

"You'd be surprised what people will do to get what they want."

Marge placed the cream and sugar on the counter and waited for him to continue. When he didn't add anything, she pushed a slice of bread toward him. "I can only imagine." Their brief conversation led her to believe there was more to it. She tilted her head and asked, "Were you having an exceptionally bad day the first time you were here?"

He broke off a corner of the dessert and chewed. "Maybe...yes. It wasn't the first time I'd been here." His shoulders drooped with the release of a sigh. "My wife and I stayed here for our fortieth anniversary." He took a sip of coffee. "She's been gone ten years now. Coming back here hit me harder than I thought it would."

The disclosure pained Marge. Of course he was upset. Who wouldn't be? Grief manifests itself in different ways. She could relate to that. "George has been gone twelve years. We came here for our twenty-fifth. That's part of the reason I loved the idea of restoring the place."

Leroy tilted his head to the side. "What's the other part?"

"We'd always wanted to open a bed and breakfast together, but it never happened. When my brother suggested we buy the lodge, I jumped at the chance to fulfill our dream—and to fill a void in my life."

She hadn't planned such a personal admission to a stranger. After Ashley's talk the other night, she started to recognize most of her commitments were based on trying to keep herself from being alone. She'd taken in college triplets a few years ago when Mutzi married Sam and moved out. Of the three girls, only Ashley still lived with her. Chelsea had moved to London and Brandi changed colleges after she had been attacked at the gold mine. Although Ashley had accepted a position as co-manager of the lodge upon graduation, Marge worried she'd move out on her own. The house would again be empty and she'd be even more alone.

Leroy nodded and offered his plate for another slice of bread. "I still work so I don't have to be at home by myself. You'd think it'd get better after all these years."

The commonality touched Marge. She gnawed on her bottom lip. Should she offer to meet him for lunch sometime? Would George mind?

No. I don't mind.

Her late husband's voice was as clear as if he were there. Before she could think more about the idea, the door swung open and Chuck stood on the stoop scraping his shoes.

"I didn't hear you pull up." She hurried to the cabinet, removed a mug, and poured her brother a cup of coffee.

"This is Leroy, the inspector." Her hand shook as she set the coffee down.

Lines creased Chuck's forehead. "You're early."

Leroy shrugged. "I knew you were on a tight schedule, so I took my chances you'd be ready for me." He passed the clipboard to Chuck. "You and your sister did a fine job fixing everything. Passed with flying colors."

Marge watched the irritation on Chuck's face ease.

Chuck glanced at the paper and nodded. "That's great. Really great." He removed the signed permits from his pocket and handed them to Marge. "I received approval from the council board this morning. Now that we passed inspection, it looks like Skipping Stone Lodge will open on schedule."

She did a little dance and waved the form high above her head in delight. "Hooray!" Marge glanced at Leroy. A broad grin edged across his face. "You should wear that smile more often. It looks good on you."

Heat rose up her neck the moment the words left her mouth. *What in the world made me say that?* As if some bold new side of her needed to take control, she continued, "Please, come to our Grand Opening on Sunday."

Leroy's smile faded. "Nice of you to offer, ma'am." He stood and picked up his clipboard. "I should get going."

He tipped his head and added, "Thanks for the hospitality," then walked out.

Once the door closed, Chuck spoke. "He's a man of few words. That exit seemed abrupt."

Marge shrugged, took the dishes to the sink, and then moved toward the door. She sensed Chuck watching her.

He came to stand by her side. "Did I interrupt something?"

She continued to watch the van pull away. "No. Not really."

"You sure?" Chuck lifted Marge's chin. "That look says otherwise."

She nodded as a tear traveled down her cheek. Marge brushed it away. "He reminds me so much of George. Same crusty disposition hiding a tender heart. Even wears the same cologne." Marge closed her eyes, engulfed in the memory of her deceased husband.

Chuck pressed a hand on her shoulder, jolting her from the moment.

"Hate to interrupt wherever your mind is, but what else do we need to do before Sunday?"

Back in the present, she drew in a shaky breath. "Good question. I better call Mutzi to find out how many have responded to the invitations." She took the cell phone from her apron pocket and pressed two for her speed dial. George's cell phone number still held number one.

Chapter Seventeen

The warm late afternoon sun bore down on Chuck's head. He examined the way the shrubs lined the south perimeter of the lodge, pleased with what he saw. Buddy had done a fine job, other than leaving the trimmer leaning against the back wall.

The snap of a tree branch drew his attention to the woods. Shadow bound toward him, and stopped short of knocking him to the ground. He rubbed the dog's head. "About time you came around. Bet you're hungry."

The black Lab turned, his ears lifted, and he peered at the thick row of oaks. His tail pounded Chuck's leg in excitement. Buddy emerged from the woods, picking cockleburs from his shirt as he meandered toward Chuck. "I finished my chores."

"Nice job." Chuck wiped sweat from his brow and picked up the trimmer.

Buddy snatched it. "Sorry. My bad." Holding the tool close to his chest, he said, "You look hot. I'll put away the trimmer. Why don't you go on in?"

"Okay. But when you're done, we're going to talk." Chuck intended to ask him about the disappearing act. Now seemed to be as good a time as any.

Shadow followed Chuck into the kitchen. Minutes later, Buddy joined them. After washing and drying his hands, Buddy downed a glass of water and turned toward Chuck. "You wanted to talk to me?"

Chuck pulled out a stool and motioned for Buddy to sit, too. "Rose Ellen texted while I was at the Planning Board meeting. Care to tell me why you took off when the police arrived?"

Buddy compressed his fingers and cracked his knuckles. "I didn't want them to find me."

Obviously. "Who's *them*?" For a moment, Chuck studied the young man's face. Was he a man or a boy? "Your parents?"

With a head shake, Buddy responded. "No. They wouldn't care if I ever came back." He glared at Chuck. "And I won't go back. No matter what."

Chuck winced. The words said with such determination spoke volumes. "The cops?"

With his chin nearly touching his chest, Buddy answered, "Maybe." He looked up with pleading eyes. "There was a truant officer looking for me a while back."

Chuck's eyes widened as he stared at the long hair hanging over the kid's face. "How old are you?"

Buddy stood and stepped away from Chuck before answering. "I'll be seventeen in December." Pleading eyes met Chuck's. "All I have to do is stay hidden two more months; then they can't do anything about it."

Chuck scratched his head as he contemplated the information. It never dawned on him before now the kid might be underage. His face bore the emotional scars of someone much older.

Pleading eyes met Chuck's stare.

"Just two months. That's all I need."

Two months. What would it take to keep him from the authorities for eight weeks? On one hand, no one else had to know his true age. On the other, the boy needed his education. There were alternative ways to get a high school diploma. *But that would require revealing his identity, wouldn't it?* "Let me think about this."

Parishioners knelt, waiting for their turn in the confessional. Mutzi lingered in the vestibule, looking out the window to keep an eye on Midnight, who slept on the church steps, his leash tethered to a railing, and a bowl of water near his furry head.

She'd waited until the last person left and entered the face-to-face door. Some folks still hid behind the curtain, as if Father Mitch didn't recognize them by the sound of their voice. It seemed silly to her. She'd come to know the pastor as a special friend.

"Bless me Father, for I have sinned." She skipped saying it had been a week since her last confession and jumped right into admitting she'd cursed three times, quarreled with Marge, had been angry with Sam, and scared Midnight in the process. Taking a deep breath, she added, "I'm sorry for storming out the other day." She pressed her lips tight and swallowed. "I'm struggling with Sam being gone all the time, and I took it out on you."

"I can see you're troubled." The pastor leaned his chin against his palm. "I can't intervene with your husband's obligations."

"I know." Admitting it out loud hurt.

"Being a deacon takes a great deal of commitment from both of you. We've talked about the importance of *your* role in this matter. Are you ready to be a deacon's wife?"

There was no sense lying to Father Mitch. It would just mean another trip to confession.

"No, I'm not...but I am trying." The words she'd spoken to Sam earlier struck home. *Try harder.* Guilt washed over her.

"The bishop won't ordain him without my support. Right?"

"That's right."

Silence filled the small room. *I'm sabotaging Sam.* That's not what she'd intended to do, but it was exactly what she'd done. How could she be so selfish? He deserved so much more than she'd been giving him. It was time for that to change.

"My dog's waiting outside. He'll be getting restless. I need to go. Better give me my punishment."

Father Mitch shook his head. "It's called penance, Mutzi."

She knew the word would rile him, but teasing, even her priest, lightened her somber mood. It's how she's always dealt with emotions. A sheepish grin found her face. "Yeah. I know."

The smile faded as she recited her Act of Contrition.

After giving absolution, Father Mitch added, "God forgives your sins."

She stared at her pastor, her friend. "Do *you* forgive me?"

The question seemed to stun him. "Of course. Who am I not to?" He sighed. "You know, *His* forgiveness is all that matters."

She nodded and stood to leave. "I'll come by next week...if you want...to teach you how to use the computer. Maybe we can talk more then."

He smiled. "I'd appreciate that. I'm available whenever you need me."

Her footsteps echoed through the empty church on her way out. As she untied Midnight's leash, a brisk breeze whipped across her cheeks and made her shiver. The temperature had dipped significantly since she'd gone into the church and an early frost was predicted. "Good thing we got seat warmers. Gonna need them tonight."

She held the truck door open and waited for Midnight to settle, then climbed behind the wheel of her truck. With a glance at herself in the rearview mirror, she said, "You can do better. So, do it."

Chapter Eighteen

Sunday morning, Chuck patrolled the perimeter of the lodge with a blower whisking any errant leaves from the walk while his three sisters busied themselves inside, making sure trays of snacks overflowed. Over the course of the morning, every accent pillow had been fluffed, and the smudges left by Shadow's nose had been buffed from all the windows.

Finished with his task, Chuck walked to the shed and pulled open the door to drop off the blower. A shaft of light penetrated the darkness and reflected off an unfamiliar coffee tin tucked behind a power saw. Curiosity drew him closer. He lifted the can and looked inside.

"What the heck?" He removed a thick wad of crisp green bills and fanned them. Dozens of Ben Franklins waved back. His hands shook as if he'd been caught in a forbidden cookie jar. *Where did this huge stash come from?* The sound of a car crunching gravel caused him to fumble the money. A few bills fell to the floor and he picked them up, stuffed them back into the tin, and returned it to where he'd found it.

Chuck's pulse raced as he made his way to the front of the lodge. He watched the first of several vehicles slow as Buddy stopped each driver and pointed them toward the recently mowed field, just as he'd been instructed. He was the only other person who normally accessed the shed. *Did Buddy have something to do with the money? Where would he have gotten that kind of cash?*

It took every ounce of control not to charge across the field and question the boy. This wasn't the right time, especially when he saw the cobalt-blue convertible roll past the teen and up the drive. Chuck squeezed his fingers into fists and released them, trying to calm his nerves, then walked over to the Mustang. "Hey, Sandi. Glad you made it." He offered a hand as she climbed out.

She studied his face for a moment. "What's going on? You look like you lost your best friend. But here I am." A half grin followed her greeting.

Chuck forced a smile. He wished she couldn't read him so easily. "Just a little nervous about the opening." He lied and released her hand. The last time he'd held it too long, she'd confided it made her uncomfortable, reminding him they were business partners, not romantically involved.

While she seemed to enjoy flirting and teasing with him, it apparently ended there.

To his relief, Marge joined them before Sandi could interrogate him further.

"Can you believe this is really happening?" Marge's eyes gleamed.

"Of course I can. The Dahlonega Sisters always succeed." Sandi glanced at Chuck and winked. "Their brother's going to too."

Marge looped Sandi's arm around hers. "This wasn't even on our radar until you and Chuck saw the possibility. Thank you for believing in me...in us."

"I'm always here for you. You're my bestie." Sandi glanced toward the lodge. "Sorry, I can't stay long. How about giving me a quick tour?"

"I truly appreciate you making the long drive from Atlanta." Marge's voice trailed off as she led Sandi inside.

When Chuck walked through the front door, Mutzi offered him a brochure. "This place has great accommodations. You should consider staying here." She laughed heartily.

Taking the paper, Chuck rolled it and bopped Mutzi on the head. "You're so silly." He wandered toward the fireplace, still thinking about the unexplained money in the shed. His thoughts were interrupted when Sam and Roberto approached, holding beers.

"Congratulations. Looks like it all came together." Sam offered an unopened brew.

"Thanks." Chuck twisted the cap off and took a swig.

Mutzi's voice rose above the murmur of other guests. She greeted each one, handed them a brochure, and then repeated her colorful explanation for the purpose of the lodge and its name. It surprised him how professionally she'd spoken until—as if she was unable to be serious a moment longer—he heard her add a finishing touch.

"At the end of your stay, we'll throw you in the river." A giggle and an apology followed. "Just kidding. You'll skip a stone across the water, and you'll leave feeling better."

"She's something else," Chuck quipped with an eye roll.

Sam shook his head. "That's one way of putting it. Not everyone enjoys her sense of humor, but she keeps me laughing—most of the time."

Taking another swig from his bottle, Chuck nodded and then glanced at Roberto. "Where's Rose Ellen hiding?"

Roberto snickered. "My wife—hide? Not a chance. She's showing someone *the* 'boudoir'." He pointed toward the hall leading to the bedroom Rose Ellen had redesigned.

"She's really proud of it." Chuck tipped his bottle to his lips.

"She told me about investing in the lodge." Roberto nudged Chuck's shoulder. "Thanks for giving her a new project."

Chuck nearly spewed his brew. Either his sister misunderstood when he said he didn't want, nor need, her money, or she hadn't been forthcoming with her husband. Either way, he chose not to get into a discussion about it today. Instead, he added it to his stash of other concerns...like the unexplained tin of money and Buddy's underage issue.

Across the room, Marge struggled to carry four glasses of champagne. "Excuse me, guys. Duty calls." He handed his empty beer to Sam and hurried to help Marge. "Let me take a couple of those." With two flutes in hand, he followed her across the room to where a group from the Dahlonega's Woman's Club had gathered.

Once the drinks were distributed, Marge turned to Chuck. "Thanks. Would you mind helping Ashley in the kitchen? She needs someone to refill the veggie trays."

"Yes, ma'am. More veggie trays coming up." He offered a butler style bow and hurried off toward the kitchen. The request had been just what he needed. Something to keep his hands busy and his mouth shut. He felt like a time bomb ready to explode. If he stayed busy there wouldn't be time for him to dwell on the other issues.

Ashley, unaware of Chuck's arrival, sang out loud to an unfamiliar rock tune, swaying side to side while she filled platters with cookies, mini quiche, and petit fours. Chuck noticed the ear buds and tapped her shoulder. She jumped, then turned and pointed to the walk-in cooler, and continued her performance without missing a beat.

"Grab some of everything," she shouted.

Inside the cold storage unit, Chuck gathered bags of broccoli, carrots, celery sticks, and cucumber slices. Once his arms were full, he tried to push open the door with his foot. It didn't budge. Applying a hip bump proved ineffective, too. He dumped some of the items onto a shelf and searched for the emergency release button.

Flashing lights drew Marge to the bay window. A sheriff's police car had stopped outside the lodge door. *A little dramatic for such an occasion, but Jack does like to command attention at times.* He'd once told her it was one of the few benefits of his job.

With a tall glass of sweet tea in hand, Marge strolled to the door to greet her friend. Her eyes widened when she realized it wasn't Jack.

"Corporal Duke." He refused the offered drink. "Here on business." The officer stood firm, one hand on his holster. "Chuck Hansen. Where is he?"

A flash of heat surged to Marge's cheeks. "Oh, for heaven's sake. What's this about?"

"Just tell me where I can find him."

Before Marge could respond, Rose Ellen intervened. She took hold of the officer's arm and urged him away from the front door. "Let's stay outside where it isn't as noisy."

The officer obliged and Marge trailed close behind the two, her mind spinning with concern.

Rose Ellen folded her arms and spoke in a hushed voice. "I told you not to come back without a warrant."

Marge strained to hear his response.

The officer whipped out a few papers and shook them in Rose Ellen's face. "Get him now...or I'll tear this place apart."

Marge's heart thumped harder. She placed a hand on her chest and inhaled, releasing a slow, steady breath, determined not to faint again. She hadn't noticed Mutzi, Sam, and Roberto had joined them.

Sam stepped between Rose Ellen and the officer. "There's no need for threats." Sam reached for the papers, but the officer snatched them back.

"I want Chuck Hansen"—the officer stuffed the papers into his pocket—"now."

Sam turned to Marge. "Do you know where he is?"

"In the kitchen, helping Ashley."

A small crowd, led by Thelma, the town's biggest gossip, had spilled outside onto the porch. Word of Chuck's detention would spread faster than honey on a hot biscuit. Marge extended her arms and pleaded, "Please go back inside. I'm sure this is a big misunderstanding." Her legs trembled as she spoke.

Mutzi tugged on Thelma's arm. "Come on. Let's go find Chuck."

Thelma hesitated, then turned and pointed to a young man in khaki pants and a polo shirt inching his way off the porch. "You might keep an eye on Johnny Ray Studdard. He's not in uniform, but he's been doing a summer internship with the force, and I saw him snooping around out back."

The guy turned and sprinted down the steps and across the parking field. Sam and Roberto exchanged glances and jumped into a nearby golf cart. "We'll be back," Sam called over his shoulder.

The corporal charged inside the lodge. Marge hurried behind him as he twisted through the crowd of guests in the great room and pushed his way into the kitchen. He whipped open the pantry door. Finding no one, he approached the walk-in freezer and yanked the door just as it flew open.

Chuck stood shivering on the other side. "Whew. It's cold in here." He smiled at Marge and shook his head. "Couldn't get out, but then I remembered to hit the emergency button."

Corporal Duke grabbed Chuck's arm, bent it behind his back, and snapped a cuff on his wrist. "Chuck Hansen. I'm taking you in."

"For what?" Chuck's eyes darted from the officer to Marge.

She had no answers. "I don't know. He won't tell me anything."

"You have the right..."

Chuck hung his head and shook it. "This cannot be happening. Not today."

Chapter Nineteen

The high-strung young corporal had refused to provide any information regarding the probable cause for Chuck's arrest. The belief that it was required was a misconception he'd learned along his painful journey with the law.

Still, by the time they arrived at the police station, Chuck seethed with the unexplained interruption to the grand opening of the lodge. Why had they brought him in?

A few minutes after their arrival at the police station, the sheriff walked in. Chuck had met him previously when he'd been unjustly accused of stealing from the Consolidated Gold Mine and attacking Brandi.

Jack tossed his hat on the desk and folded his arms across his chest. His steely blue eyes drilled the deputy. "I'm gone for twenty-four hours. All you were supposed to do was stay here and monitor the phone. What the hell's going on?"

The green-horn cop couldn't talk fast enough. "He's the burglar from the Crisson Gold Mine heist."

The sheriff glared at the young man and shook his head. "What have you done?"

He thrust his cell phone into his boss' face. "I ran the plates. His truck was in the parking lot that morning."

"No way." Chuck countered. The end of the news story he'd heard about an incident at the mine surfaced in his memory. "I've never been to that gold mine."

The sheriff glanced at the phone, and then ordered the officer, "Put him in a cell, then come to my office."

The guy whose name tag read Duke grabbed Chuck's arm and tugged him down a hall with a snarky smile plastered on his face. "You just won me a promotion, mister."

"You've got the wrong guy."

"That's what they all say." The corporal slammed the door and left.

Chuck collapsed onto the cot. Despair stole his soul. He was innocent. Again. What was it about him that made people suspect him of such terrible things? Was this his fate?

The past continued to haunt him. Decades ago, he'd tried to help a young woman being attacked by her ex-boyfriend. He'd arrived before the cops, but too late to save her. They'd charged and convicted him of murder.

Locked away, he steadfastly proclaimed his innocence. All the while, he'd hoped they'd realize their mistake.

It took years of constant prodding to get a felony review committee to look into his case. Eventually, DNA testing proved his innocence. Yet, even after his release, he faced persecution from those who believed he was guilty. Steady employment eluded him and before long, he was homeless, living in his car.

When Sam invited him to Dahlonega, he clung to the possibility of living a normal life. Until...Brandi. Ashley's free-spirited sister lived life on the edge. She'd wanted a job and Chuck suggested the Consolidated Gold Mine. He'd warned her to stay away from the cocky manager. He sensed the jerk wanted more than naive Brandi understood. Chuck tried to interrupt the man's sexual attack, only to have the mine collapse on top of him and Brandi. Once again, the true criminal was nowhere to be seen. Chuck was in the wrong place at the wrong time. But this time, the girl survived and identified the jerk as the offender. In addition to an attempted rape conviction, the guy was charged with stealing thousands of jewels from the mine.

There was little he could do from inside jail to prove he was nowhere near the other gold mine, but if his truck was there, it meant Buddy had been. But why? He felt confident the kid hadn't robbed the place. What did he know about Buddy? He was only sixteen. Surely, he wouldn't try something so extreme. But the can of money in the shed concerned Chuck. Was it part of the stolen heist?

He refused to drag the kid into this mess unless he was sure he was involved in some way. It would mean the authorities learning his age and sending him back to a place he feared. At some point, Chuck needed to meet with Buddy, but that didn't seem likely from behind bars.

He'd been talking with Sandi when the news broke about the gold heist. She could testify to it, but he could have been calling her from anywhere. There was no way he was dragging her into this mess. She had an impeccable reputation and he refused to tarnish it any more than he already had.

What had all the years of struggling taught him? While he believed in telling the truth, his experience with the law made him hesitant to share anything. Everything he said could and would be used against him in court. No, he needed to keep his mouth shut and trust they would find the robber.

But how long would that take and who would help his sisters with the lodge opening? Would people bale on their reservations? God, he hoped not. Marge, Mutzi, and Ashley could handle the guests, but there were so many other things that required muscles, not that they wouldn't try.

Maybe Buddy would stick around and help. Sam was busy with his deacon studies, and Roberto still worked. Neither would have time to help keep the grounds trimmed and firewood cut. Besides, Chuck held the responsibility for all the financial obligations that needed to be attended to. Sandi's name was on the bank accounts, but dumping the extra work on her wasn't right.

Stale beer found its way to the top of his throat, and he struggled to keep it down.

Chapter Twenty

Roberto's curator duties required him to return to Atlanta in the midst of the turmoil at the lodge. Rose Ellen fingered the edge of the drapes as she glanced out the window and watched her husband drive away. She turned and realized her sisters watched her from the great room. "He needs to retire soon. I thought we'd spend more time together once we got married. After our extended honeymoon, he went right back to a full-time schedule."

"He must enjoy his job and it probably makes him feel productive." Marge patted the armrest of the chair next to her. "Come join us."

"Maybe he needs to get away from you." Mutzi snickered as she picked up a votive candle and swirled the liquid around and around, sending a wave of the sweet vanilla scent through the room.

"Mutzi!" Marge's voice rose to a warning level.

"She knows I'm just kidding." Mutzi tossed a pillow at her older sibling. "I'm in the same boat she's in. Sam's always gone and I don't like it one bit."

Rose Ellen caught the pillow and eased onto one of the comfy chairs near the fireplace. Maybe her sister was right. What if *she* was the reason Roberto refused to retire? Once, during a heated argument about the cost of the house renovations, he'd said he couldn't afford to support a high-maintenance wife without the steady income. She'd have to give it more thought, but not now. Now, she had other concerns to distract her.

"Where is Sam now?" Marge asked Mutzi.

"He drove to the police station to see if they'd let him talk to Chuck."

"Jack said he couldn't have any visitors yet."

Rose Ellen stared at the dwindling fire. "Our grand opening was a fiasco, and quite embarrassing. At least Sylvia had already left before everything went down with Chuck." Rose Ellen didn't wait for a response from her sisters. "There is one positive aspect...for me, at least."

Mutzi leaped from her seat. "You're unbelievable! This isn't about you and your high-society friends. Our brother is in jail...again. For who knows what."

The unexpected reaction stung. Rose Ellen pressed a hand to her chest. Misjudged. Again. She decided to remain calm and continue to make her point. "If you let me finish, I think you'll understand."

Marge reached out and urged Mutzi to sit back down. "Let's hear what she has to say."

"Thank you." Rose Ellen said, "As you know, April hasn't practiced law since Savannah was born. Recently, the firm she'd worked for offered her a new position. She wants to take it, but can't find a sitter she trusts." Rose Ellen folded her hands on her lap. "I've decided to babysit my granddaughter."

Marge and Mutzi exchanged wide-eyed stares.

"You don't think I can do it?" Rose Ellen cocked her head.

"It is a serious commitment, Sis," Marge confessed. "I'm not sure I could do it. Savannah, any toddler, is a handful and hard to keep up with. Besides, there's quite a distance between your house in Atlanta and April's condo in Dawsonville. How would that work?"

Rose Ellen held up a finger. "I've got it all figured out. It won't be easy, but I'm in good health and I think I can do it. I'll make a schedule of activities to keep Savannah busy. She still takes a nap every day, so I can rest when she does." The idea had been simmering in her mind for a week. She felt more confident about her decision to become her granddaughter's nanny as each day passed.

"As far as the commute, I'll stay at April's during the week. It will be best for Savannah to be in familiar surroundings, and her parents will be close enough to check on her whenever their schedules allow. Roberto's working long hours, so I doubt he'll mind. And besides, absence makes the heart grow fonder, right?"

"That's very...thoughtful...and generous." Marge glanced toward Mutzi. "Quite considerate of our sister, don't you think?"

Mutzi twisted her mouth. "Surprisingly so. But I don't get what it has to do with Chuck's situation."

"I've been contemplating it for a week, but today's debacle solidified my decision. Our brother's going to need an attorney. They are expensive and Chuck's finances are already stretched to the limit. April helped him before, and I'm sure she'd offer her services again."

In truth, caring for Savanah full time by herself scared the daylights out of Rose Ellen, but she knew it was the right answer to the current situation.

Marge stood. "I think this deserves a group hug."

Rose Ellen and Mutz joined her. The three held firm for a moment, pumping unexpected confidence into Rose Ellen. A calm washed over her. *I can do this.*

In her usual "I'm not a hugger" fashion, Mutzi squirmed and stepped back, then poked Rose Ellen's arm with a finger. "Who knew my spoiled-brat sister had a good heart?"

Unable to resist the tease, Rose Ellen responded, "Don't forget. I was Dad's favorite."

With a quick retort, Mutzi quipped, "Well, if he'd known Chuck was his son, I bet we'd all have been further down his favorite kid list."

The suggestion made Rose Ellen laugh. "You're probably right."

Marge smiled and then grew serious. "Let's get focused on how to help Chuck." She pulled out her phone. "I want to talk to the sheriff. Maybe Jack can shed some light on what's going on. I'll ask him if we can come talk to Chuck."

"While you do that, I'll go in the boudoir and run my decision past April." Rose Ellen waved her fingers as she left the room.

"Guess that leaves me to look for Buddy. Maybe he knows something we don't." Mutzi left through the front door.

Chapter
Twenty-One

Marge paced around the great room while she spoke with the sheriff on the phone. "Come on, Jack. You know as well as I do Chuck didn't rob the gold mine."

"A photo of his truck in the parking lot the morning it happened might suggest otherwise."

"Oh, my." Marge stopped and eased onto the couch. "Did he explain why he was there?"

The sheriff paused. "He swears he's never set foot on the place. Says someone else had his truck, but he won't give me a name."

How strange. Who would Chuck trust enough to turn over the keys to? If it was Buddy, why wouldn't he just tell the sheriff?

The unanswered question would have to wait until she talked with her brother. There *was* one question Jack could answer. "I'm really hurt you chose to make the arrest at our grand opening. Why?" Her normal fondness for the sheriff had soured because of the timing of the arrest. She'd always respected his discretion in doing his job and never knew him to purposely embarrass anyone.

Jack cleared his throat, and his voice lowered to a whisper. "I'm sorry. I just got back in town this afternoon. If I'd known what they were up to…"

"They? Who are they?" Marge fumbled the phone, but caught her cell before it could fall.

"Nothing. Forget what I said."

"Pretty hard to forget when my brother was dragged out of here in handcuffs in front of our potential guests."

Silence. Anger built while she waited for a response. The pressure in her chest felt much like it had just before she fainted a few days ago.

Get control of yourself.

She closed her eyes, drew in a deep breath, and let it escape her lips like a pinhole in a balloon.

"Are you still there, Jack?"

"Sorry. I have to go."

The call ended. Determined to not let the unanswered questions steal more of her time, she tucked the cell into her pocket and willed herself to get to work, packing up the leftover food. Despite her intention, the conversation continued to replay in her head. If Jack hadn't instigated this, who had? And how would they benefit from Chuck being in jail?

An unfortunate incident which took place last year came to mind. Just before the grand opening of a new bed and breakfast, the owners were forced to declare bankruptcy when the final permits got stalled for months because of political bureaucracy. An out-of-town company swooped in and bought the place for pennies on the dollar. Changes in the city's approval process were made to prevent it from happening again, but what if...the idea was too upsetting to consider. She shoved the thought away.

Marge's eyes grew wide when she walked into the kitchen and found the marble island bare. "For goodness sakes!" The stove, sink, and every counter glistened.

Ashley stood near the island and grinned. "Time for you to sit. The leftovers are in containers in the fridge and everything else is in its place except the last load in the dishwasher."

Marge pressed a palm to her own cheek. "Oh, honey. I didn't expect you to put everything away by yourself."

"You've had enough stress for one day. I'm glad I could do something useful." She dangled a set of keys. "I hope you don't mind. My sisters are in town and want to meet for dinner tonight. I'd like to go to the house and shower before joining them."

"Mind? I'm overwhelmed with how much you've helped. You're an angel." Marge squeezed the young woman's hand. "You deserve a week off, but you know that's not possible with our schedule." They exchanged hugs. "Go. Enjoy your evening. Give my best to Brandi and Chelsea."

Ashley wrinkled her freckled nose. "I know this whole mess is upsetting. Wish I could help more, but remember what the Bible says. I think it's John 8:32. The truth will set Chuck free."

"You really are special. Thank you. I needed the reminder."

"You're welcome. Now, please sit." Ashley waited until Marge obeyed, and then she left.

Every nerve from Marge's shoulders to her feet, screamed for a break. With her elbows on the island, she rested her head on folded hands, closed her eyes, and drifted off.

A noise startled her awake. She jumped from the stool and glanced around the room as she gathered her bearings. It took a moment to realize someone had knocked on the back door. A knowing smile lifted Marge's face. *Leroy.* She'd been disappointed when he didn't show at the grand opening, but it hadn't surprised her. "Come in."

The health inspector stepped inside, removed his tweed herringbone hat, and wiped his shiny oxfords on the mat. "Didn't want to barge in unannounced." The corner of his mouth raised. "Ma'am."

She watched him fiddle with the collar of his crisp white shirt, pleased he'd made the effort to dress up for the special occasion. "I'm glad you stopped by," Marge greeted him as she gripped the fridge handle. "I could use a glass of tea. Would you like one?"

Lines creased Leroy's forehead as he nodded. "I thought your grand opening was from noon until four." He placed his hat on a counter and checked his watch. "I planned my arrival to help with cleanup."

A tentative smile built when his words sunk in. Once again, he reminded her of George. He would have done the same thing. She removed a pitcher of tea from the refrigerator. "That was very thoughtful." She poured two glasses and set them on the island. "Unfortunately, it ended prematurely when"—the words caught in her throat—"when an officer took Chuck to jail." She swallowed hard before adding, "They think he robbed the gold mine."

The lines deepened on Leroy's forehead. "I'm...sorry. I..." He snatched his hat and held it close to his chest. "I should probably leave."

"No." The word blurted out. Being alone with nothing to clean or cook increased the anxiety already settling in Marge's heart. "Please. Stay."

Leroy kneaded the rim of his hat. "If you're sure. I'm a good listener if you want to talk."

His offer was appealing. Yet, she worried the unsettling news about the arrest might dampen their budding friendship. Most people didn't want to be involved with family drama. On the other hand, if he truly was like George, he could be supportive, and she needed all the support she could find right now.

Her stomach's loud growl filled the silence like a cough during a solemn church service. "Oh, goodness. That was embarrassing."

His smile produced a dimple. "I bet you were so busy you forgot to eat today."

She nodded. "You're right." Pointing to the walk-in refrigerator, she added, "There are a ton of leftovers. How about selecting a couple of sandwiches for us?"

Leroy strode across the room and pulled on the walk-in's handle. It didn't budge. With the second yank, the door released. "That new seal's a bit tight."

Marge hurried to his side. "Let me hold the door while you go in. Chuck got stuck in there earlier." The painful flashback overwhelmed the momentary joy of Leroy's visit. She sniffed and reached in her pocket for a tissue. "The officer thought he was hiding."

Leroy met her eyes and placed a hand on her arm. "Anything I can do?"

"Not unless you know who the real crook is." The cold air from the cooler sent a shiver down her spine. She pointed to his left. "Chicken salad croissants would be nice." Each one had been individually wrapped. She sent a silent *thank you* to Ashley.

With two bundles in hand, Leroy elbowed the door. "I've got it from here."

Marge released her grip and crossed her arms to rub the chill away. "Is it too late in the day for coffee?"

"Not for me. Sounds good." He set the food on the island. "I'll get paper plates and napkins. They're in the pantry, right?"

"Yes." Having a man helping in the kitchen pleased her. Leroy's shoulder brushed Marge's as he came out of the pantry and a tingle shot up her body. The scent of musk blended with a hint of cinnamon caused her to linger with nostalgia. *Same aftershave as George.*

"Did I forget something?"

Leroy's voice nudged her back to the present.

"No. No. I was thinking." She couldn't possibly tell him what she was really thinking. Instead, she turned and went back to the pantry. "Something crunchy would be good, too." She selected a package of lightly salted potato chips and a tin of her homemade cookies. "I think we're ready."

He stepped back and offered her the lead. "Ladies first. Always."

She tipped her head. "A true gentleman. Thank you."

Leroy pulled out a stool for Marge, then sat on the one next to her.

They exchanged glances as they unwrapped the sandwiches. Marge's shoulders relaxed. "This is nice."

Just as she took the first nibble, her sisters charged into the kitchen.

"Whose truck is that?" Rose Ellen demanded.

Marge tried to swallow, then grabbed her napkin to cover her mouth as she choked. She'd forgotten her sisters were still at the lodge.

Leroy sprang to his feet. He appeared torn between helping Marge and wanting to flee.

Marge took a sip of tea and motioned for Leroy to sit back down. He remained standing.

With raised brows, Rose Ellen inquired, "Who's this? Another hired hand I didn't know about?"

Marge set her napkin down and stood. "Meet my sisters, Mutzi and Rose Ellen." Her eyes met Leroy's. "He's the county food inspector and also a good friend."

A curve of a smile lifted Leroy's cheek. "Perhaps it would be best if I leave."

"I don't see why you should." Marge glanced from one sister to the other.

Mutzi laughed. "Okay with me. How about you, Rose Ellen?"

With a shrug, Rose Ellen offered a nod.

His eyes met Marge's. "If you're sure." Leroy returned to his seat.

Mutzi reached for a chip from Marge's plate.

Marge slapped her sister's hand. "You know better than to do that."

"I'm hungry as a bear." Mutzi looked at her older sister. "I bet Rose Ellen is too."

The gracious person in Marge made the offer. "The sandwiches are in the walk-in-refrigerator. I'll get a couple and you can join us." The selfish part of her wanted to send the two away so she could spend time alone with Leroy. Marge started to stand.

Mutzi interrupted. "Sit. We can get our own food."

Rose Ellen released a harrumph, but Marge complied and insisted Leroy do the same.

Once everyone settled, Mutzi stared at Leroy. "So, your duties include tasting the food, too? I want that job." She chuckled.

Marge decided to change the subject. "I talked with the sheriff."

Both her sisters leaned in.

"Apparently, they have proof Chuck's truck was parked in the gold mine's lot the morning of the heist."

Rose Ellen dabbed her mouth with a napkin. "I didn't think Chuck was *that* desperate."

Mutzi elbowed Rose Ellen hard enough to bump her off the stool. "I can't believe you would even think that about your brother."

Rose Ellen lurched to the side and grabbed the island to keep from falling, then sat back down. "I was joking."

"Didn't sound funny to me. How about you, Marge?" Anger burned in Mutzi's eyes.

"No. It wasn't funny." Marge glared at Rose Ellen. "Chuck says he's never been there and I believe him." She rubbed the back of her neck and glanced at Leroy. His poker face held firm.

"I believe him, too." Mutzi stuffed a chip in her mouth and crunched. "Can't believe they'd get a judge to sign a warrant based on so little."

Rose Ellen barked, "I can't believe they'd embarrass us like they did."

"Jack...the sheriff...said if he'd been in town, it wouldn't have happened that way."

The room grew quiet. Everyone seemed lost in thought. The conversation with Jack replayed in Marge's mind. What did Jack mean by that? Unwilling to spend more time dwelling on the unsettling statement, she passed the tin of cookies to Rose Ellen and asked, "Were you able to reach April?"

"Yes. She's going to make some calls." Rose Ellen slapped a hand on the marbled-island. "Can you believe April didn't jump at my offer to care for Savannah so she can return to her practice?"

Marge and Mutzi exchanged glances. The responsibility of watching a toddler all day might be too much for any seventy-year-old, much less her self-absorbed sister, but Marge kept the thought to herself. Instead, she suggested, "Maybe April just needs time to think it over. Going back to work is a big decision."

Leroy stood, gathered the empty paper plates from the table and disposed of them. "I should go and give you ladies some privacy." He raised a hand to stop Marge. "Please, don't get up. I can let myself out."

When he leaned in close to Marge, her shoulders tensed. *Is he going to kiss my cheek?* It's not that she would have minded. But doing it in front of her sisters? She wasn't quite ready for a public display of affection.

Instead, he reached into the tin and snatched another snickerdoodle. "One for the road, if you don't mind." After retrieving his hat from the counter, he nodded toward Rose Ellen and Mutzi. "Nice to meet you both." To Marge he added, "I'll be back tomorrow to help, if you want me to."

"I'd like that." She watched as he slipped out the back door. When he was gone, she turned to find her sisters staring at her.

Rose Ellen nudged Mutzi. "I do believe our sister has a gentleman caller."

Heat rose up Marge's neck. "Stop it." She brushed a hand through her hair. "We need to focus on Chuck."

Chapter Twenty-Two

Mutzi stared out the window as Sam drove them home. The tall oaks cast creepy shadows on the road. She lowered the window a bit for a wisp of fresh air, taking in dusk's earthy scent. "I can't believe the sheriff wouldn't let you see Chuck."

Sam shook his head. "They have procedures to follow, hon. I should have realized it would be a waste of time going there." He reached across the seat and patted her hand. "Maybe we'll learn more tomorrow. If April agrees to represent him, they should let her see him."

Too many problems weighed heavy on Mutzi's heart. Chuck's arrest and the future of the lodge eclipsed yesterday's concerns regarding Sam's mission to become a deacon. Would she and her sisters be able to manage the lodge without Chuck? Marge, Ashley, and she could manage the guests. If Buddy stuck around, he'd take care of most of the maintenance of the facilities. But Chuck had the educational degree needed for all the responsibilities of running a business, especially paying the mortgage and other bills.

Thoughts of Buddy competed for her attention. When she'd found him after Chuck's arrest, he'd told her how he'd been beaten by his father nearly every day of his life. His story stirred an unfamiliar motherly love in her heart. The need to protect him from further pain wrapped around her soul and squeezed.

Thank goodness her sisters hadn't asked about the kid. Mutzi had found him sitting on a stump near the river, ironically in the exact location the lodge guests would spend the final day of their sojourn.

Potential guests, Mutzi corrected herself. After today, she wondered how many would cancel their reservations. Six had prepaid and were scheduled to arrive on Thanksgiving. They'd leave on Monday. She, Marge, and Chuck had decided the benefit of a brief first booking would allow them to test the waters and make adjustments for the next group, who were scheduled for the week of Christmas. They'd wanted to offer a respite for people who found the holidays a difficult time.

"Honey," Sam's deep, soothing voice interrupted her thoughts. "Want to talk?"

She shook her head. It was too much to put into words. Buddy had confided in her about the abuse he suffered at the hands of his father and the reason he ran whenever he saw authorities. She'd promised not to repeat his story, even to Sam, unless it was absolutely necessary. Her heart ached for him.

Another, stronger emotion boiled inside her. Anger. She couldn't understand why the officer had decided to make a big scene at the grand opening. Was it a mistake by an inexperienced cop or was someone trying to frame Chuck? Jack's comments made Mutzi wonder who initiated the warrant if the sheriff wasn't in town.

She studied Sam's profile and asked herself another question. Her best friend, a wise man who helped her overcome crazy superstitions, sat right next to her. Why wasn't she taking advantage of the limited time with him? Who better to share her concerns with than her husband?

"Didn't you find it strange the sheriff wasn't there when they arrested Chuck?" She folded her arms tight. "The entire situation reeks."

Sam shrugged. "Marge said he was out of town."

The ugly event churned in Mutzi's gut. "What judge would sign off on a warrant if all they had was a picture of Chuck's truck?"

"I thought it was odd the officer wouldn't let me see the warrant." Sam rubbed his chin. "It's almost as if—"

Without waiting for him to finish, Mutzi blurted out, "Maybe that rookie didn't *have* a signed warrant. But why would he pick on Chuck? Today? Someone wanted to sabotage the lodge."

Sam glanced at her, then back to the road. "Do you really think so? Why now?"

"It's the perfect time!" Mutzi straightened in the seat and turned toward Sam. "The permits are in place. All the dirty work is done. It's the perfect time for someone to swoop in and take it over. Just like they did with the bed and breakfast last year."

The suggestion hung in the air for the next mile.

At the last stoplight in town, Sam asked, "Who would benefit if the lodge failed?"

"I don't know, but I'm sure as hell going to find out." She mentally tasked herself with another confession to Father Mitch for cursing.

The moment Sam pulled into the garage, Mutzi sprang from the truck and beat a path to her computer.

Chapter Twenty-Three

"We need to stop meeting like this."

The unexpected greeting jolted Chuck from his distant thoughts. Rose Ellen's daughter, April, dressed in a navy-blue power suit, stood outside his jail cell. A brilliant lawyer, devoted mother, and his lifeline to freedom, shared a half-smile.

"I didn't expect you to come. Thanks, but…" While seeing her lifted Chuck's spirits momentarily, reality wiped away the hint of hope. With the financial strains of opening the lodge, he couldn't afford her services. She'd handled his previous case pro bono. Doing it again wouldn't be right. "I appreciate you intervening, but I can't afford to hire you, April."

With a headshake, she answered. "I'm not looking for money. I'm here for justice. I know for certain they've got the wrong guy."

He didn't deserve her kindness. He didn't deserve to be in jail, either. Is this what the rest of his life would be like? Accused of one crime after another? The constant battle drained him. It strained his friends and his family. "My poor sisters. The last thing they need is the stress of a brother who keeps landing in jail. And Sandi. I can only imagine the negative publicity she'll receive from being partnered with a criminal."

"Try to trust the system, Chuck. I know it failed you in the past, but it does work right most of the time. I'm here to make sure of it."

"I don't know what to say." He ran a hand through his hair. "Thank you."

"Why don't you tell me what you know?"

Chuck gnawed on the inside of his cheek. How much should he tell her? Now was the time to decide. Should he confide about Buddy? He'd promised to protect the kid, to not let anyone harm him. Would the Department of Family Services send him back to his abusive father or a foster care situation? Would they charge him with stealing Chuck's truck? Did the kid even have a driver's license? None of that would happen if he kept his mouth shut about Buddy.

However, he had to get out of this mess in order to be of use to the boy and his sisters.

"I've never been to that gold mine, but apparently a photo proves my truck just happened to be there the day of the heist."

April didn't blink. "Who was driving it?"

He drew in a deep breath and released it. "There's this guy, a kid really, living on the streets. Broke my heart—you know I've been there. I offered him a place to stay and meals if he helped me at the lodge." He closed his eyes. "I didn't know a damn thing about him. Put my sisters and the lodge at risk and now I'm stuck in here. He's a good kid. I believe in my heart he's innocent."

"You didn't give the sheriff his name because you're protecting him. From what?"

Chuck rubbed his day-old beard. Sharp as a tack, this woman was. He liked how she cut to the chase. "Years of physical and mental abuse aged the kid. I thought he looked to be nineteen or twenty. Never would have guessed sixteen."

"Runaway?"

"I guess. He didn't reveal his age until after he'd returned with the truck. He begged me to not tell anyone since he'll be seventeen in just two short months."

"Did he take the truck with your permission?"

"Sort of. The day before, I told him how pressed I was for time and needed more mulch to finish a job. He'd been asking to drive my truck and suggested he could not only get the mulch but at a good price to boot. Without realizing what I'd agreed to, I said sure.

"The next morning, I overslept and when I went looking for Buddy, he and the truck were gone. Freaked me out. I didn't remember the conversation we had until he came back with the mulch and reminded me. That's when he pleaded with me to not turn him in."

April nodded as she made notes. "So, you didn't report the truck stolen?" She paused. "The sheriff was in a generous mood today. He provided a clue as to why they are still holding you. Where did the hundred-dollar bills come from?"

The question jolted Chuck. "How do you know about the money?"

"They confiscated it from the shed at the lodge. The serial numbers match some of the money taken from the gold mine."

Chuck's stomach roiled. "I don't know how it got there. I found it just as guests started to arrive at the grand opening." Another thought landed a punch to his gut. His prints would be all over the bills he'd thumbed through. "I can't believe Buddy would be involved in any of this. That's not the kid who's been helping me out these last couple of weeks."

"They confiscated your boots, too. Buddy wore them?"

Chuck nodded. "Damn. What have I gotten myself into?"

"The best chance you have of getting out of here is to tell them about Buddy. You know that, right?"

He sucked in a deep breath. "Then the kid gets locked up." He stared at April as he struggled with the obvious conclusion. "Maybe he's innocent too. Maybe this is a wrong place, wrong time situation."

"Maybe. But can you really afford to continue to protect him? Apparently, he's made some bad decisions. It's possible he's involved with the burglary. Do you really know him well enough to risk losing the lodge and being convicted of another crime you didn't commit?"

Everything she said made sense, yet he knew how the system worked. Buddy could be tried as an adult, and if convicted, he'd never be able to shed the record. Even as a juvenile, the experience would leave a lasting mark on his mind regarding authority.

"I need to talk with Buddy. He's the only one who can explain all this."

"That's not possible without revealing his identity. Would he be willing to talk to me?"

Chuck shook his head. "I don't think so. I doubt he'll trust anyone, especially now." He thought for a moment.

"Maybe Mutzi. He seemed to have a special connection with her."

"Bottom line. Your guests will be arriving in two days and my aunts need you at the lodge. Is it fair to them to delay this?"

The question hung in the air like a dark, rain-filled storm cloud. Could he, should he throw Buddy under the bus? If so, what were the chances the kid would ever have a normal life? Chuck sure hadn't enjoyed one.

"I'm not ready to give him up. My gut tells me Buddy is as innocent as I am. He's a kid who needs help, not more trouble."

April frowned. "I'll talk with Mutzi. But until you're ready to identify Buddy, there's nothing else I can do."

Chapter Twenty-Four

After hearing from April, Mutzi returned to the lodge around daybreak the following morning. She'd left in a rush, unprepared for the significant temperature drop during the night. She opted to wear one of Chuck's camouflage jackets. It hung past her knees and she worked to fold back the extra six inches of sleeves that engulfed her petite arms.

Shadow paced by the front door of the lodge. His nails clicked the hardwood floor while his black tail thumped the wall, sending an SOS message to hurry. "I'm coming. Give me a minute." Satisfied she'd done the best she could with the coat, Mutzi opened the door.

"Do your thing and then we've got a mission to accomplish." She'd hoped the strong bond Shadow displayed with Buddy would help her find him. Neither Marge nor Mutzi had seen the boy since the evening of the grand opening. Food missing from the refrigerator led them to believe he hadn't run off too far and they had hoped he'd return soon, but April's call to Mutzi made it more urgent to talk with him and find out why he'd taken Chuck's truck to the gold mine.

She had no clue where he might be, but if he was on the property, the dog would find him. Maybe he would trust her enough to share his side of the story.

Shadow emptied his bladder, then looked at Mutzi.

"Where's Buddy?" she asked. As she hoped, he bound toward the thick woods. He weaved around thorny bushes and towering oaks. Then he slowed, his coal black nose sniffed the ground, and he broke into a gallop. Mutzi scrambled to keep the canine in sight. She considered herself agile, but could not match the fast pace of the Lab. Just when she thought she'd have to stop to catch her breath, Shadow slowed and yelped twice.

The elusive runaway stepped from behind a massive tree. The eager dog pounced on him with such force they both tumbled to the ground. Mutzi watched from a distance not wanting to interrupt the amusing scene. The unconditional love between the two warmed her heart.

"Whoa. Take it easy." Buddy struggled to his feet and tugged on his dirty worn sweatshirt with one hand while he continued to stroke Shadow with the other. "I guess you missed me."

Mutzi closed the gap between them. "We've all missed you." She pointed to a nearby log. "Let's sit. We need to talk."

The tangled hair and dark circles under his eyes hinted at the troublesome days Buddy had spent hiding.

"They haven't let Chuck out yet?"

"No. Not yet." She picked up a twig and broke it into little pieces. "He seems to think you have some information that might help."

"I didn't mean to get him in trouble. I was trying to protect..." The boy stopped mid-sentence and his eyes widened.

From the flush which crept over Buddy's cheeks, Mutzi sensed he'd said more than he'd intended. "Who? Who were you trying to shield?"

He blew out a held breath. "I promised not to tell."

Her neck stiffened. "Buddy. Sometimes keeping a promise does more harm than good. This is one of those times. We can't let Chuck sit in jail for something he didn't do. He needs your help more than whoever you're trying to protect."

"But she'll be mad at me—and all of you will be mad at her."

Mutzi bristled and squeezed her fingers into a fist. Only one person fit that scenario. "Rose Ellen?"

His eyes answered her question.

"She asked me to help her...with something." He hung his head. "When the cop car showed up, I panicked."

Mutzi nodded. "I get you didn't want the officer to find you. But what did Rose Ellen want from you?"

"A truck delivered furniture before she arrived one morning."

Mutzi jumped up, arms flailing like a boxer. "I knew it. She lied to us."

Buddy covered his head with his arms.

Realizing she'd frightened him, she stilled. "I'm sorry. I didn't mean to scare you. Our family doesn't hit. Ever." She sat back down on the log. "Just tell me what you know so we can get Chuck out of jail."

He seemed to study Mutzi's face as if trying to decide what to say. "She'd ordered tables and lamps. They were really expensive pieces, but they didn't match any of the furniture in the great room. I helped her hide the new stuff in the shed. She said she couldn't return it without you guys knowing. I said I knew a guy who would buy it."

By the time he finished his story, Mutzi believed she had enough information to clear Chuck of the charges. Now she needed to find a way to keep Buddy from paying the price of his naivety. "Walk with me to the lodge. Marge has made a big pot of chili. Bet you're hungry."

His eyes lit. "I'm starved!"

When they reached the front door, she motioned for him to go in. "Please let Marge know I'm going to town to talk with a friend." She patted him on the back. A plan inched its way into her thoughts. "Don't worry, Buddy. Everything's going to be all right."

A phone call to April confirmed what Mutzi had hoped. The information Buddy shared should be enough to convince the sheriff to release Chuck. It might even lead officials to the person who stole the money from the gold mine.

She parked next to the pastor's car in the church parking lot and walked inside. Her spirit lifted as she looked around his office. The piles of paper which had been stacked in every corner and on the two swivel chairs had dwindled. Father Mitch glanced up from his keyboard and nodded.

"Have a seat, Mutzi. I'll be right with you."

More hopeful than she'd been in days about getting Chuck out of jail, she playfully spun the empty chair around a few times and then sat. "Looks like you're getting pretty good with the computer."

"Still got a way to go, but it's much better. Thanks to you." After a few more taps, he stopped. "What can I do for you today?"

"How would you like to have a teenager helping out at the rectory for a few weeks?"

Father Mitch's brows drew tight as he leaned forward, resting his chin on a fist. "What's the catch?"

Mutzi let out a belly laugh. "You know me too well."

She grew serious. "Suppose there was a kid who ran away from an abusive father, and without realizing it, got himself into a jam. Could the church offer him protection?"

"Depends on what kind of a jam he got himself into." The priest reached for a book from the shelf and flipped through a few pages, and then paused.

Every nerve in her body wanted to tell him what she'd researched the previous night. Still, the decision was at his discretion, and she didn't want to offend him with her eagerness. Mutzi pressed her lips tight as she waited.

He raised his head and met her eyes. "Tell me more about this jam the kid has gotten himself into."

Chapter Twenty-Five

The familiar white van pulled close to the kitchen door and stopped. Marge walked outside and greeted Leroy with an appreciative smile. It was the third time he'd been to the lodge this week. The pile of firewood multiplied, not a single weed disturbed the flower garden, and the aging shed boasted a lovely forest green coat of paint, all thanks to Leroy's help.

Marge felt bad about asking him to do one more chore, but with Chuck in jail and Buddy still hiding, she'd made the call asking him to come by. "You're a saint. The delivery guy dropped this huge bag of dog food right here. If it stays outside overnight, every animal within ten miles will find it, including the mice."

"I'm not ready for a halo, yet." He hefted the fifty-pound bag over his shoulder. "Where do you want it?"

She nibbled on her bottom lip. Making him carry the heavy bag all the way to the shed bothered her, but not as much as storing it in the kitchen did. "Chuck mentioned a metal container in the shed. I think that's where he usually keeps it."

"Smart man." He shifted the weight on his shoulder as he turned. "Lead the way."

Marge hurried down the step and around the back of the lodge with Leroy inches behind her. Startled to see the shed door open and garden tools scattered on the ground, she stopped abruptly. Leroy bumped into her and sent her tumbling to the ground.

"Oh, my gosh!" He dropped the bag and hurried to her side. "Don't move."

He crouched down next to her. "I need to check to make sure you haven't broken anything. Are you okay with me touching you?"

He met her eyes, apparently waiting for her approval. The familiar musky scent of his aftershave stirred an unexpected desire to touch his face. The strange thought made her look away. The instinct to get up and brush off his offer passed when a sharp jolt of pain made her wince. She gulped and nodded for him to proceed.

His strong, work-weathered hands moved down one arm, then the other. The warm touch sent a shiver up her spine.

"Arms look okay." He continued with her left leg and then the right.

She rolled to her side and heard a snap. Another stab of pain made her yelp. "Ow!" She closed her eyes and said a silent prayer. *Please Lord, don't let it be a broken hip.*

Leroy paused. "That sounded like something broke. I think we better call for an ambulance."

"No. I've got too much to do. I'm fine. Really." She pressed her hands on the ground and pushed herself up. After she sat for a few moments, she decided to try and stand. "I'm getting up."

"I really wish you wouldn't."

"Oh, I'm going to get up. With your help or not. I'm not going to lay here and wait an hour for paramedics to arrive and tell me I'm okay."

Leroy shook his head. "Stubborn as all get out. Just like my late wife." He stood close by with his arms stretched to help her up. Once she was on her feet, he pointed to the ground where she'd been laying. "Maybe that's your broken bone."

She glanced down and noticed the fragmented tree branch. "I think you're right. Thank you, Jesus." Out of the corner of her eye, she saw Buddy race toward them, Shadow a step ahead of him.

"Miss Marge! Are you okay? What happened?"

"I'm fine." She glanced toward Leroy and grinned. "I was attacked by a fifty-pound bag of dog food."

With a wink, he retorted. "Not my fault you have no brake lights."

Buddy's brow wrinkled. "But *are* you okay?"

"I think so." She lifted her right leg and wiggled her foot. "My ankle is a little tender, but I can manage."

Buddy picked up a rake and shovel from the ground.

Marge folded her arms across her chest. "What were you doing with all this stuff?"

"Sorry." He kicked at a clump of dirt. "I was organizing it, and then had to go to the bathroom."

"Please put it all back into the shed and the dog food, too."

"Yes, ma'am."

Leroy offered an elbow to Marge. "At least let me walk you inside...or I can carry you."

Heat warmed her face. "I'll walk. Otherwise, we'd probably both be on the ground." She gripped his arm and hobbled back to the lodge.

Chapter Twenty-Six

Savannah ran from one room to another with Rose Ellen struggling to keep up. The eighteen-month-old proved to be more of a challenge than her grandmother had expected.

When she sprinted into the kitchen, Rose Ellen leaned on the counter and panted. She glanced at the clock, grateful it neared noon. "Time for a break. How about a peanut butter and jelly sandwich? That's your favorite, right?"

A delightful squeal accompanied the tiny pitter-patter of bare feet on the hardwood floor. "Nonna!" The strawberry blond tot wrapped her arms around Grandma's legs.

Rose Ellen lifted her into the high chair and grabbed a wipe to clean her hands just as her cell phone rang. She glanced at the screen. "It's your Aunt Mutzi. Wait until she hears what we're doing." Rose Ellen tapped the speaker button. "Busy, Sis. What do you want?"

"Ha. I bet you've got your feet up enjoying a cup of coffee on the patio."

"You'd lose that bet. I'm babysitting Savannah and that leaves no time for sipping coffee. Although I could use a caffeine fix about now."

"That's right. I forgot. April told me she was giving you a trial run."

"Run is right. This little cherub never sits still."

"Hate to spoil your fun day, but we need you at the lodge."

"I couldn't possibly—"

"Yes. You could. It was your idea to be included in this adventure."

Rose Ellen finished wiping Savannah's hands. "What's the emergency *now*?"

"Marge fell and twisted her ankle. I'm heading there. Bring Savannah with you. Marge can entertain her while we work in the kitchen. See you in a couple of hours."

The call ended before Rose Ellen could protest. She stood there staring at her granddaughter, trying to remember what she was doing when the phone rang.

Savannah pounded the tray on the high chair. "Poo but."

Rose Ellen cringed. Did she really need to go to the bathroom again?

The little girl continued to pound her tiny fists on the tray. Her voice elevated. "Poo but."

A light bulb went off in Rose Ellen's brain. "Peanut butter! Sorry, kid. I forgot."

She hurried to finish making the sandwich and poured milk for both of them. Savannah, who normally used a sippy cup, giggled as she picked up the glass and some of the liquid dribbled out the sides of her mouth.

"You are a little devil, aren't you?" Rose Ellen wiped her chin and settled onto a chair, grateful for the brief rest.

Ten sticky fingers and an empty cup later, the child pounded the tray again. "Down."

"That one I know." Nonna helped Savannah from the chair.

Mutzi's phone call replayed in Rose Ellen's head. Being part of the lodge *had* been her idea. The opportunity to prove to her siblings she was serious had presented itself. Could she manage watching Savannah and helping out at the lodge? Only one way to know for sure.

"Looks like you'll be napping in the car seat today, young lady."

With Savannah balanced on one hip, Rose Ellen glanced at the diaper backpack and her oversized Louis Vuitton purse. "How am I supposed to carry all this and you too?" Should she secure the baby in the car seat and return to the kitchen for the other items or do the reverse? Savannah giggled again, apparently entertained by Rose Ellen's indecision.

Doubt edged into her thoughts. What had she been thinking when she offered to babysit? Was she too old to manage watching her granddaughter *and* helping at the lodge? Should she call April and tell her to come get her daughter? With a head shake, she sat Savannah on the counter and weighed her options.

The assessment took only a minute. She refused to give her sisters the chance to say "I told you so."

Rose Ellen studied the situation. "How did I do this when April was little?"

After she'd caught her no-good spouse cheating, the sole responsibility of raising her daughter rested on her. Not only did she succeed in that effort, she'd even managed to open her own boutique in New York, juggling a job and motherhood quite well. A woman who could do all that surely could handle a road trip with her granddaughter.

She eased Savannah to the floor and pointed a finger at her. "Stay put for a minute." She swung the strap of the backpack over her left shoulder, her extravagant purse over her right, and reached for Savannah's tiny hand. "I can do this. I am woman!"

The child squealed as they walked to the car. "Go bye-bye."

As she neared the car, she heard the door unlock, thankful for the key fob stashed in her purse. Savannah scurried into the car seat April had secured in place—in case of an emergency, she'd said—when she dropped the girl off earlier. Meanwhile, Rose Ellen tossed the backpack on the floor and dropped her purse on the empty passenger seat.

Rose Ellen stared at the car seat straps, trying to remember how to secure her granddaughter in place. She tugged, pulled, and pushed until she heard the latch click.

"See how smart Nonna is?"

Once settled behind the wheel, Rose Ellen pressed the start button and the engine hummed to life. With the eighty mile drive down GA 400 underway, she breathed a sigh of relief.

Soft music from the radio lulled Savannah to sleep within fifteen minutes. Rose Ellen began to relax until another thought occurred. What if her daughter came early to pick up Savannah?

"Call April." Rose Ellen waited for the hands-free mobile service to dial.

"Hey, Mom. How's it going?"

"Very well. Savannah ate all her lunch and now she's napping." With any luck, April wouldn't know she was driving. Rose Ellen would tell her later, after they'd arrived safely. Best to ask for forgiveness than permission.

A four-by-four truck tailgated close behind, and when the driver decided to speed around, he blew his horn and shook his fist.

Rose Ellen cringed, knowing April would hear the blast.

"Mother!" her daughter shouted. "You're in the car."

Gripping the steering wheel tight, she answered, "Yes."

Panic rose in April's voice. "I told you I didn't want you driving her anywhere unless it was an emergency."

Rose Ellen resisted the gut reaction to shout back at her daughter. Instead, she said, "Hush. You're going to wake your daughter." A glance in the rearview mirror confirmed Savannah didn't hear her mom. "This *is* an emergency. Marge fell. We're on our way to the lodge."

"Oh, no. How bad is she hurt?"

"I'll let you know when I get there." Determined to prove she could handle a crisis while watching her granddaughter, she ended the call with a quick, "I'll call you later. Bye."

With each mile that clipped away, Rose Ellen's confidence grew. She'd prove to everyone she was capable of being a doting grandma. Being a caretaker wasn't new to her. Memories came flooding back.

When their mother died, although Rose Ellen wasn't even a teenager yet, caring for Marge and Mutzi became her responsibility, especially when her dad traveled. They had just started kindergarten. At first, getting them ready for school, feeding them, and making sure all their needs were met made her feel important. She'd bossed them around as if she were an adult. As days turned into years, resentment replaced the pride she had felt. While teenage friends partied and had fun, household chores and parenting consumed her days.

Upon graduation from high school, she'd been quick to accept her boyfriend's proposal. His grandiose ideas of moving to New York enthralled her and provided an escape from motherhood.

It didn't take long before she realized being married wasn't much different than being a nanny to her sisters. Not only did she have the same responsibilities for all the cooking, cleaning, and serving her husband, now she had to manage the bills on a meager budget.

The first time she suspected her spouse of cheating, he swore he was working late, but his paychecks never reflected extra hours. In a bold attempt to save her marriage, thinking it would keep him around, she became pregnant. Instead of strengthening their relationship, he'd left her for another woman three months before April was born.

Rose Ellen's heart hardened and she vowed never to be anyone's doormat again. She demanded more from life than being a maid, cook, and a snubbed wife. A survival attitude blossomed within her until she no longer saw herself as a victim, rather a prize to be won by anyone who wanted her attention. After the divorce, she scrimped and saved every penny she could and with the small investment she'd managed to stash away, she started a brick and mortar and later moved it to an online boutique.

Rose Ellen glanced in the rearview mirror and watched Savannah snooze. She'd teach her more life lessons and prepare her for the real world, just like she'd done for April. Being Savannah's caretaker would provide that opportunity.

Chapter Twenty-Seven

Leroy's suggestion to create a list of the final tasks which needed to be done before the guests arrived proved to be a good distraction for Marge. She'd have preferred to do the work herself and know it was done right, but he'd convinced her to stay off the ankle for the rest of the day. There was almost nothing she could accomplish from the couch.

Her limited mobility ruled out the Beef Wellington she'd originally hoped to serve for their family dinner tonight. Flipping through the recipe box Leroy had brought from the kitchen, she settled on her own version of Burgershire soup. Surely, her sisters could manage a simple pot of soup. Scanning the ingredients, she nodded and raised her eyes to Leroy. "Would you mind getting two pounds of ground beef out of the freezer?"

"No problem." He extended his hand. "If you give me the card, I can get all the other components together"—a smirk spread across his face—"and maintain your orderly cabinets."

She cringed at the thought of Mutzi and Rose Ellen rooting through the cupboard and disrupting her systematized shelves. She trusted Leroy to preserve her desired order. "That would be wonderful." She offered a smile. "I can't believe you took off of work to help me, again. You are one of the most thoughtful men I've ever known. I don't know what I'd do without your help."

He chuckled. "My vacation goes unused almost every year. Besides, considering I'm the one to blame for knocking you over, it's the least I can do."

Marge tsked. "It was an accident. I shouldn't have stopped so suddenly." The reminder stirred her concern about the mess of tools left on the ground by the shed. "Did Buddy put everything back?"

Leroy nodded. "I checked a little while ago. The area looks great."

"I wonder what the boy was looking for?" She continued to fret about Chuck, Buddy, and the soon-to-arrive guests. Marge rolled her shoulders and pressed a hand inside her collar to ease a knotted muscle.

Leroy frowned. "Is your neck hurting now?"

"Not from the fall. Really. I'm okay. Just anxious about...things I can't fix."

"Your stress gravitates to your shoulders." He moved closer. "Just like my late wife. She always said my strong hands were perfect for a massage. Want me to try one out on you?"

She delighted in the inviting offer, but what if her sisters walked in? "I imagine she did appreciate those...moments. Maybe another time." A blush heated her cheeks. "The burger really needs to start thawing."

His eyes glistened and he stepped back and turned toward the kitchen. "Another time."

The ornate grandfather clock chimed two times. Marge heard footsteps come through the great room.

Mutzi called out, "I'm here, Sis. Where are you?"

"In the kitchen." Marge perched on one stool and propped her foot on another. An orderly arrangement of celery, carrots, onions, and spices lined the island.

"You did all this on one foot?" She poked a finger at the swelling in Marge's ankle. "I thought you were staying off of it."

"I have been sitting on the couch all morning." She swept a hand across the potpourri of items. "Leroy arranged all this."

A mischievous grin spread across Mutzi's face. "So, how did you really hurt your ankle? Was there some hanky-panky going on?" A playful chuckle followed.

Marge slapped her sister's arm. "Shame on you." The inappropriate suggestion reinforced her earlier decision against Leory's offer for a massage. "He is a true gentleman. He's been a blessing helping me with chores Chuck would normally do."

Mutzi rubbed her arm. "Yeh. He seems like a nice enough fellow." She picked up the recipe card and eyed each ingredient on the island. "He must be anal retentive...like you." She stepped far enough away to avoid another smack.

The fact that Leroy shared the same need for order pleased Marge. "He went to the bakery to get some bread for dinner."

"Hard to believe Skipping Stone Lodge opens for business tomorrow." Mutzi rubbed her hands together and stepped close to the island. "I guess I better get started on this soup."

Marge's stomach clenched. Even though it had been years since Mutzi nearly burnt down her kitchen, memories of it always surfaced when her sister decided to cook. "Didn't you say Rose Ellen was on the way? Do you want to wait for her?"

Mutzi thrust her hands on her hips. "You never forget. One little fire and you hold it over my head the rest of my life."

"I just thought you two would like to work on the soup together." Marge gnawed on her bottom lip. Her sister knew her too well. It was true. The memory of the damage she'd caused to the Victorian house her husband had built still lingered strong.

"Fine. I'll wait for precious Rose Ellen...who doesn't cook any more than I do." She glared at Marge. "What else needs to be done?"

Marge handed her the pad of paper. "Would you mind double-checking all the bedrooms and bathrooms to make sure we haven't missed anything?"

Buddy eased through the back door, nodded toward Marge, and then hurried out of sight.

Marge frowned. "That was strange."

Mutzi shrugged. "I saw him before I came in and asked him if he'd cleaned his room. Guess he decided he better do it." With the list in hand, Mutzi marched out of the kitchen. "See you later. If I don't come back, it's your fault because I'll be taking a nap."

"Thanks, Sis." Marge thought a nap sounded pretty inviting. Unable to sit any longer, she lowered her injured ankle and squirmed off the stool. A glance out the window revealed a truck coming toward the lodge. She recognized it. Sam? What in the world was Mutzi's husband doing here so early?

He parked and entered through the back door.

"I wasn't expecting you until later this evening. Is everything all right?"

Sam didn't answer. Instead, he said, "I thought you were supposed to be elevating that foot."

"I have been." She pointed to where she'd been sitting. "I couldn't take the stool any longer." She studied his face. It was unlike him to circumvent a question. What now, she wondered.

"Come on. I'll help you to the other room." He slipped an arm around Marge's waist. "Lean on me."

The two made their way into the great room where Marge settled on the couch with a subtle groan. What wasn't Sam telling her? Mutzi must have known he was coming, since he didn't ask for her when he came in. *More bad news?* Otherwise, he'd have answered her. Her nerves, already maxed from worry, raised to a whole new level. She wrestled with a throw pillow that wouldn't conform to the shape she wanted. Frustrated, she threw it across the room.

"Guess you showed that cushion who's boss." Sam picked up the discarded object from the floor, perched on the end of the couch, and held Marge's hand. "It's going to be okay. Everything is going to work out just as it was meant to be. Trust in Him." He offered a gentle squeeze and stood. "Perhaps an ice pack and some ibuprofen would help, too."

Marge dabbed a tissue under her eyes, anticipating the few tears might turn into a flood. "I hope He's listening." She scooted sideways and propped her foot on the end table. She watched Sam disappear into the kitchen. He returned with the cold compress, a glass of water, and two pills.

She decided to approach the unanswered question again. "I didn't realize you were coming early today. What's going on?"

"I'm on a special mission. I won't be staying, but if all goes well, I'll be back later with some good news."

Good news? Marge sure could use some of that. It pained her heart not to have Chuck here when guests arrived. He'd spent a year preparing for the lodge to get underway. It just wasn't fair.

She turned when Mutzi entered the room, followed by Buddy, who had a backpack slung over his shoulder.

"I'm ready." He walked toward the sofa, dropped the pack, and wrapped an arm around Marge. "Thanks for making me feel like family."

Marge gasped. She glared from Buddy to Sam. "What's going on? Where are you taking him?"

"A safe place. I promise." Sam focused his attention on Mutzi. "We need to go...*now.*"

Mutzi fist-bumped Buddy. "You've got this, kid." She pulled him into her arms and squeezed.

Marge stared in disbelief. What was happening?

Buddy stepped back and picked up his pack. "I have to do this...for Chuck."

The words choked from Marge's throat. "Come back soon. We need you here." Her heart shattered as the two walked out. Uncontrollable sobs followed.

Mutzi handed her sister a box of tissues and patted her shoulder. "Don't cry, Sis. Buddy's going to be okay. He'll tell the sheriff what he knows, which should get Chuck out of jail. I've tried to make sure Buddy has a safe place to go to until this mess is resolved."

Marge blew her nose. "It's all so wrong. Neither of them deserves this. They're good guys."

"I know. Someone needs to pay for all the crap they've put Chuck and us through." Mutzi walked toward the kitchen. "Rose Ellen's still not here. I'm going to start making that soup."

Before she could dissuade her sister again, Marge's cell phone rang. A glance at the screen showed Sandi's name. She answered with a shaky, "Hello."

"Happy almost Thanksgiving!"

A sob caught in Marge's throat. "Thanksgiving? Oh, no."

"What's wrong?"

"Everything!" Marge blubbered. "I forgot to thaw the turkey. How could I forget to do that?"

"Don't beat yourself up over it. I bet you could whip up something else instead."

"I can't even stand up for five minutes." She sobbed into her tissue.

"You're hurt? What happened?"

When she stopped crying enough to respond, she said, "I fell and twisted my ankle."

"Is anyone there to help you?"

"Mutzi came...and...Sam was here, but he's gone. He took Buddy to the sheriff's office." Marge howled again. Her normally well-planned, organized world crumbled into tiny pieces like a shattered glass beyond repair.

"Marge. Stop crying. You've faced worse catastrophes and weathered through it. We'll fix this, too. I'll be there as soon as I can."

The guilt of dumping on her best friend troubled Marge. "You don't need to do that. I'll be okay."

"Of course I do. Just sit tight."

Just sit tight. That's all she'd been doing and it wasn't helping. She pushed herself up from the couch and limped to the kitchen to check on Mutzi.

Chapter Twenty-Eight

With the heavy traffic behind her, Rose Ellen decided to exit the highway and find some place to grab a cold drink. Savannah stirred awake just as the car pulled into the parking lot of a quaint road-side market.

"Hello, my little sweet pea. Did you have a good nap?" Rose Ellen turned off the engine and climbed out, shutting the door behind her. She rolled her shoulders and stretched her legs.

Savannah squirmed in the back seat, trying to free herself from the seat restraints. "Nonna. Out! Me, too."

"Hang on a minute. Nonna's coming." Rose Ellen walked to the other side and pulled on the handle. It didn't open. A jolt of reality caught her breath. "Oh, no!" She glanced at the designer bag, which took up the entire front passenger seat of her 2016 Nissan and groaned. The only access to her keyless entry vehicle lay inside the purse.

Her frustration skyrocketed when she realized her cell phone accompanied it there. What in the world was she going to do? Her only option was to go inside and ask for help, but it meant leaving Savannah alone and out of her sight.

Savannah's bottom lip puckered and she began to wail. "Out, Nonna."

"I'm sorry, honey." Rose Ellen placed the palm of her hand on the window. Guilt and a sense of fear rose and settled in her chest. "Nonna will come right back."

She hurried inside, shouting as she opened the door, "Help! I need help!"

The cash register sat unattended. "Hello. Anyone here? I have an emergency." Her voice quivered and she feared she'd start crying, something she never resorted to. She raced down the bread aisle and up the house goods row. Dread intensified when she reached the rear of the market. Just then, a petite, white-haired woman emerged from behind a rotating rack of lace doilies.

The woman's muted green eyes widened as she stumbled back and placed a frail hand on her chest. "You gave me a fright. I didn't hear you come in."

Rose Ellen started to suggest she add a chime on the door to announce customers, but she didn't have time to waste on such an obvious fix. "I need your phone. It's an emergency."

The five-foot fragile store keeper shook her head and took off toward the front of the building. "We don't have a phone."

Rose Ellen followed. "I don't believe you. Everyone has a phone nowadays. I need to call the police."

"Go away. I don't get involved in drama."

"My precious granddaughter is locked in my car. Please, let me use your phone."

The woman folded her arms and looked out the front door. "I told you I don't have a phone."

How could a person be so coldhearted? Rose Ellen wanted to scream and shake her into reality. Instead, she dashed back to her car and tugged again on all four doors, praying one would open. "Don't cry, Savannah. I'll get you out." The little girl's chest shuddered as she gasped between wails. *April will be so angry with me.*

After racing around in a panic, Rose Ellen wiped perspiration from her forehead. She gave thanks the temperature was only in the mid-fifties, so Savannah wasn't roasting in the closed car. She noticed a car coming and quickened her step while waving frantically in hopes to catch the attention of the driver. A woman in the passenger seat waved back, but the car sped by.

The distant hum of more tires approaching urged her to a more urgent approach. She stepped into the street and held up both hands up while she squeezed her eyes closed and dared the next driver to stop or run her over. She held firm and listened for the car to screech to a stop. Relieved when it did, she peeked out of one eye and released her breath.

A young man with unruly red hair leaned out the window and yelled louder than the rock music blaring from his radio.

"Get out of the road, lady!"

"No! I need help. *Now*." She moved closer to the window for him to hear her better. A glance into the souped-up Chevy revealed crumpled fast-food bags and empty soda bottles strewn all over the floorboards and passenger seat. "What a mess."

"Hey, you wanted help, lady, don't judge." He reached over and turned down the volume. "What's up?"

"My granddaughter is locked in the car and I can't get her out."

His eyes widened with concern. "Yikes. Move aside." With that, he whipped his Chevy into the parking lot. He jumped out, holding a long metal tool in his right hand. "Slim Jim to the rescue."

Rose Ellen wiped away a tear that trickled down her cheek as she watched the redhead wiggle the metal piece down the window frame. Her eyes drifted to her terrified granddaughter. A few seconds later, she heard the lock click.

"There you go." Red opened the door and pressed the unlock button. "Suggest you stay out the middle of the street, lady. The next guy might just run you over."

"I will," Rose Ellen answered, still in shock over how quickly he managed to complete the task.

"Thank you!" She unbuckled Savannah and pulled her into a tight hug.

The toddler pushed away. "Ow!"

"Sorry, honey." Rose Ellen eased her granddaughter to the ground. The young hero who had helped free Savannah started his engine. Rock music blared again as he sped away.

"Thank you, Slim Jim, or whoever you are," she called out.

With her purse retrieved from the front seat and slung over her shoulder, Rose Ellen held Savannah's hand and led them into the store. "Let's get you something cold to drink."

The child's face, wet with tears, glistened. "Pee pee."

Nonna smiled. "Good idea. We'll do that first."

She led them into the store. Rose Ellen anticipated another unpleasant interaction with the shopkeeper. "I dare her to tell me she doesn't have a bathroom. If she does, you can go pee pee on the floor."

Savannah giggled as if she understood her grandmother.

Chapter
Twenty-Nine

Let's go, Hansen." The sheriff unlocked the cell door. "You're cleared."

Chuck stared at Jack. Through his past experiences, he'd learned the importance of words. "Cleared? What exactly does that mean?" Held without bond, released on one's own cognizance, charges dropped, bail posted—he knew and understood those terms. Cleared wasn't one he'd heard before.

According to April's visit yesterday, charges still pended, but the seventy-two-hour limit for holding someone without an indictment expired today. Had they dropped the charges? The only visitors they'd allowed him to see were Sam and a persistent, unsolicited reporter who wanted to write a feature article about him. She'd come by several times and urged him to tell her his story. Although she seemed sincere in her efforts, he struggled with the notion and had sent her away.

Jack drew in a deep breath. "You're released. No charges pending. You're free to go."

Chuck sensed the man, Marge's good friend, held on to more information. "That's it? What do you know that you aren't saying, Jack? Is another officer going to show up at the lodge in a day or two and drag me back here for another seventy-two hours? Do you need more time to drum up more false charges?"

Jack shook his head. "No. If I have anything to say about it, it's over as far as you're concerned." He ran a hand through his hair and sighed again. "I know you had nothing to do with the heist. Your name's been cleared."

Anger and anguish turned somersaults in Chuck's gut. "That's the thing about being arrested, Jack. The story makes headlines, giving your office credit for taking a criminal off the streets, but when someone *is* innocent of the charges, the rest of the story is swept under the rug. Problem is, the damage has already been done and the black mark never goes away. I've never been *cleared* from any false accusations. The negative effects on my life have never been repaired. Do you know what it's like being falsely accused over and over again?"

"No. I don't." Jack handed Chuck the wallet and cell phone taken from him when he was brought in. "I'm sorry. Sometimes mistakes are made."

"A mistake? Bull. I don't believe this was a mistake. Someone set this whole fiasco up and that person needs to pay for this. You know who that is." He scowled at the sheriff. "Don't you? Who, Jack? Who?"

Jack pressed his lips tight and shook his head.

Chuck rubbed the three-day stubble on his chin and contemplated what the release from jail meant. He'd be back at the lodge before the guests arrived, but would they want him there, or would they turn away, believing the worst of him? Heck, he didn't know if any of the guests were even still booked.

Stop this nonsense and focus on the positive. Sandi's voice inched through his struggle as if she were standing next to him. He needed to focus on a more positive scenario. Perhaps the guests were still coming. April hadn't mentioned postponement or cancellation of their arrival. There were enough daylight hours left for him to finish up any chores Buddy hadn't done. *Buddy!* It hit him like a brick wall. Was Buddy the reason he was being released?

Chuck grabbed Jack's arm. "Why was I cleared?"

The Sheriff turned away. "I'm not at liberty to say." He removed Chuck's hand. "It's complicated and I can't discuss it."

"What are you afraid of? That I'll sue? You bet your ass I'm going to sue. Every stinking one of you. This is a bunch of bull crap."

The sheriff pressed his lips tight. "I can't blame you. But no one ever wins." He shook his head. "They never win."

Chuck heaved a sigh. He'd have to deal with those frustrations later. He scrolled through his phone, trying to decide who to call for a ride. April's name flashed on the screen. He swiped to answer. "Hello."

"I'm parked out front when you're ready."

He glanced out the door. April waved from inside her car.

Chuck turned his attention to Jack, his brows pulled tight in confusion. "You called her?"

The sheriff shrugged. "It's the least I could do."

Chapter Thirty

Mutzi glanced at a text which had come in on her phone at five o'clock, and then stuffed it into the pocket of her bright yellow smock with playful puppy images stamped all over it. It had been nearly a year since she'd worn the festive top, but today felt like a day worthy of a smile. Her secret plan was working out perfectly.

She turned her attention to Marge. "You look as limp as a dishrag. Why don't you lay down for a while?"

Marge shook her head. "I should be doing something, but I don't know what."

"We're all ready for tomorrow." She moved close to her sister's face and squinted. "You look like one of those shrunken apple-head dolls."

"Mutzi! That's rude." Marge pressed a hand to her cheek. "Do I really look that bad?"

The exaggerated claim seemed necessary to convince her sister to get some rest. "No. But you do look tired.

I promise to wake you in time to freshen up before the others arrive."

"I'm still worried because Rose Ellen isn't here. You don't think something happened to her, do you?"

The thought *had* crossed Mutzi's mind, but she wasn't going to add to Marge's stress by agreeing. "That broad will be late for her own funeral. I'll check with Roberto to see if he's heard from her."

Marge rose from the couch. "Maybe I will lay down for a minute."

"Good." Mutzi watched her sister hobble into the bedroom. The moment she heard the door close, she scurried into the dining hall. From the bottom drawer of the antique credenza, she removed ten pumpkin-shaped placements with matching napkins, enough for all the family and friends who should arrive by six-thirty. Even with Savannah's high chair nestled between two chairs, there was plenty of room for more. Her thoughts drifted to Buddy. She wished he could be here, but at least the supervisor at children's services had agreed to let him stay with Father Mitch.

Bright oval paper platters, printed with pumpkins, fall-colored leaves, and the word *thankful* scripted across the middle added to the mood she'd hoped to create. Marge wouldn't like the decision to use disposable products and plastic ware, but it would save time and energy later with the cleanup. Besides, the special surprise to top the evening would be enough for her to overlook such minor details.

Mutzi had just gone into the kitchen to grab extra paper napkins from the pantry when Leroy rapped on the back door. She opened it and he entered cradling three loaves of artesian bread.

She took one from his arms. "Put those two in the pantry."

The barked order brought a smirk from Leroy. "Yes, ma'am."

The back door opened again, and Sam marched in carrying a large box.

He gave his wife a peck on the cheek. "Two dozen pieces of fried chicken from the Smith House restaurant, just like you ordered."

Leroy laughed as he shook his head. "She's turned into a drill sergeant."

"You have no idea." Sam winked at his wife.

Mutzi opened the box and drew in a whiff. "Smells good."

Sam closed the lid before she could sneak a piece. "You can wait like the rest of us."

She scrunched her face, trying to look mean, then grew serious. "Speaking of the rest of us, I still can't get Rose Ellen to answer the phone or my texts. I wonder if she's stuck in traffic?"

Sam shrugged. "I didn't hear about any backups on 400."

The sound of another engine drew Mutzi's attention to the window. Leroy and Sam leaned next to her to see who'd arrived.

Roberto came inside, shaking his head. "I can't believe she's still not here." He ran a hand through thick waves of salt and pepper hair, his trimmed grey brows drawn tight with concern. "Maybe I should retrace the route. I tried to watch for her, but it's hard to do while driving and it's starting to get dark."

"Let's not panic." Mutzi wasn't ready to sound the alarm just yet, but it was wearing on her nerves as the hours ticked by. She opened the refrigerator and withdrew three bottles of beer, handing one to each of the men. "Why don't you guys hide out in the dining hall until the others get here. It will be a nice surprise for Marge when she gets up."

Sandi's blue mustang arrived next. She opened the trunk and took out three gallon-size containers. Mutzi hurried to the door to help her carry them in.

"The Dahlonega Woman's Club sent enough potato salad, coleslaw, and pork and beans to feed a small army."

Mutzi offered a towel to wipe the condensation that dripped from Sandi's arms. "They are a great bunch of ladies."

"Where's Marge?" Sandi swept a stray curl from her cheek.

"Hopefully, she's taking a nap. I think the fall and all the stress wiped her out."

"What a tough time for all of you. I'm sure glad it's almost over."

"You heard?"

"Chuck called after April picked him up. They should be here any minute. They went to Dawsonville to pick up April's husband, Paul."

"Marge doesn't know Chuck's out. I thought we'd surprise her with chicken dinner since she was so disappointed to be serving soup instead of her Beef Wellington. She won't care what we're eating once she sees Chuck."

"I can't wait to see her face and his." Sandi cast her eyes out the window.

"So, what's with you and Chuck?"

"We're partners, and friends." She twisted her ponytail as she continued to stare into the dark night.

"Friends? I'm pretty sure Chuck would like more than that."

She nodded. "I know he does. I'm just not ready...yet."

Mutzi sensed the conversation ended there. "The guys are in the dining hall if you want to join them. Need a beer?"

"No. Thanks. Think I'll wait. I've got champagne chilling in the cooler."

Mutzi opened the potato salad and took a spoonful. "The bubbly is a nice touch. Now we just have to figure out what to serve the guests for Thanksgiving."

Sandi's brown eyes widened. "I almost forgot. The woman's club also sent two fully cooked turkeys."

"Perfect. We've got all the other fixings for the guests arriving tomorrow. Marge will be so relieved."

Mutzi checked her watch again. Where the heck was Rose Ellen? If Savannah had been in the car all this time, she'd be pitching a fit.

She watched another set of lights creep down the long driveway. Mutzi couldn't see the make or model of the car, but the shadows of the passengers as they got out of the car were not those of an aging woman and little girl. Chuck, April, and Paul strolled through the door.

As happy as she was to see her brother, the knot in her stomach tightened. Still no Rose Ellen.

Chapter Thirty-One

A noisy commotion stirred Marge from her restful nap. "Oh goodness. How long have I been out?" She focused an eye and read the digital clock. Six-thirty. Had she slept all night and the guests were arriving? She jolted upright, squinting to see if the clock read a.m. or p.m.

Thankful it was the latter, she rose from the bed with caution, anticipating pain when she stood. Slowly, she balanced on one foot, and then took a tentative step with the other, gradually adding more weight to the injured foot. The minimal amount of pain brightened her spirit as she walked into the bathroom to splash a little water on her face and comb her hair.

The ruckus coming from the great room grew louder as she walked down the hall. At the sight of her brother, her breath caught. The weight of a dozen sand bags lifted from her body. "You're here!" She wrapped an arm around his waist and held tight. "No one told me you were being released today."

"I didn't know it either until April showed up." He bear-hugged Marge.

A glance around the room astonished Marge again. "Oh, my. Everyone's here. You were supposed to wake me, Mutzi."

"Sorry. We wanted to surprise you."

"You certainly did that." As she took count of the people in the room, the smile faded. "Where're Rose Ellen and Savannah?"

Mutzi stepped closer and offered a reassuring pat on her back. "She said to start without her. She's on the way. You know how our sister likes to make an entrance when all the work is done and the food is on the table." She laughed.

Marge's head was still fuzzy from the afternoon nap. One by one, her worries resurfaced, leaving a sinking feeling in her stomach. She looked out at the crowd. "I'm sorry. I wasn't able to fix a fancy meal. All we have for dinner is soup." She turned to her sister. "At least we have that, thanks to Mutzi." She remembered the frozen turkeys and her stomach dropped further. "I don't even know what we will serve tomorrow."

Mutzi patted her shoulder. "It's all under control. Let's go into the dining hall and we'll fill you in on the details."

The troop made its way into the other room. The festive table was filled with food. Happy tears pooled in Marge's eyes. "I take a little nap and you make miracles happen."

Mutzi grinned. "We've got your back, Sis. You don't have to carry the load all by yourself."

Leroy pulled out a seat. "Why don't you sit and we'll all join you."

Chairs screeched on the hardwood floors as each person found a place.

Mutzi announced, "We should probably eat before all the food gets too cold."

"We're here!" Rose Ellen shouted from the great room. The patter of little feet grew louder as Savannah raced into the dining hall.

"Mommy!" A shoeless Savannah sprinted to April and jumped on her lap, kissing her like she'd been gone for a week.

A collective sigh echoed through the room. Roberto stood and greeted his wife with a smooch. "Bellissima signora."

Rose Ellen returned the caress. "Were you really going to eat without me?"

Mutzi shook her head and released a harrumph. "Where have you been?"

A sheepish grin spread across Rose Ellen's face. "That's our little secret. Right Savannah?"

Tiny blue eyes sparkled as the girl's blonde curls bobbed. April glanced at Paul who seemed to read her mind. He picked up Savannah and put her in the highchair.

Roberto took Rose Ellen's hand and whispered something in her ear. A blush rose from her neck as she sat.

Marge's mind spun with unanswered questions. "Let's eat. When we're done, we've got a lot of issues to talk about, like where this bountiful meal came from. It miraculously appeared like loaves and fish while I napped." Marge extended her hands, Chuck on her right and Leroy on the left. "Sam, would you say grace?"

"Of course." He waited for everyone to join hands. "Heavenly Father, you have brought us together to celebrate family, for there is nothing more important than the love we share as one with You. May we remember the extraordinary blessings we've received today and carry them in our hearts throughout the coming year. Amen."

A chorus of "Amen" resounded throughout the room. Savannah echoed an extra one for good measure.

Chapter
Thirty-Two

A flurry of emotions stole Chuck's appetite as he glanced around the table at his extended family and friends. The joy of being out of jail and welcomed as part of this loving group was tempered by a shadow of guilt.

He felt responsible for Buddy's absence even though he'd done all he could by not revealing his identity to the sheriff. In the end, it had done little more than edge him closer to the age when he'd be allowed to act on his own. Where was he and how would this experience shape his future?

Regret also stirred in his heart for having brought so much turmoil to all of them, including Sandi and Leroy. They'd done nothing to deserve their lives being turned upside down by his presence. He'd often thought they would have been better off if he'd never come to Dahlonega. They'd done nothing but loved him. Was this the price they paid for doing so?

Anger, an emotion he tried never to let grip his soul, stole part of his spirit. Forgetting and forgiving were two different things. He couldn't forget being accused of crimes three times. Would he ever be able to forgive this latest infraction? It boiled in his stomach and he wanted to lash out at...whomever stirred this hornet's nest. An eye for an eye went against his principles, but dang it, it had to stop somewhere.

He couldn't ignore the anxiety that remained regarding the success or failure of the lodge. The responsibility of repaying the loan and making a profit weighed on his shoulders. He couldn't cope with the possibility of failure.

Sandi reached under the table and squeezed his hand. Her eyes locked with his and without voicing a word, she reminded him to focus on the positive.

Chuck drew in a deep breath and released it as he looked around the table. Family. Friends. He needed to thank each one of them. Where should he begin?

"I don't know what I've done to earn the love and support all of you have given to me. Bless you, each and every one of you. I appreciate it more than you'll ever know." He raised his glass and offered a toast. "To the opening of Skipping Stone Lodge and the end of all the craziness."

"I'll drink to that!" Mutzi cheered along with him. "It's been a heck of a week."

Chuck grew more serious. "Tell me about it. Please, tell me what's happened. I need to know."

"It was the biggest bungled mess Dahlonega's police department has ever seen. There's an investigation going on with that no-good group who swooped in and bought that bed and breakfast last year. Everything's hush hush, but they should be banned from doing business. Scum bags." Mutzi took a sip of water and continued. "I also have information from a dependable source that there was never a valid warrant. The rookie cop thought he'd secured a fast promotion for catching the gold mine crook. Instead, he got fired." She frowned. "I think you should sue all of them."

The thought had crossed Chuck's mind more than once. "Right now, I'm more interested in what's happened with Buddy. Where is he?"

Sam placed his napkin on the table. "We arranged a meeting with the sheriff, juvenile authorities, and Father Mitch. Buddy confessed to driving your truck and being at the gold mine the day of the robbery. Although he wasn't involved in the heist itself, he did accept payment for some goods he delivered. It turned out the hundred dollar bills he received were traced to the robbery."

The information confused Chuck. "He picked up mulch for the lodge. What would he have delivered?"

Sam stared across the table at his sister-in-law. "I believe she can explain more about that."

Rose Ellen choked on the wine she'd just sipped. "I don't know…"

Sam tilted his head, never breaking eye contact with her. "Yes. You do know. Just be honest."

She placed the goblet on the table, straightened her shoulders, and sucked in a breath. "It wasn't a big deal. He was disposing of some furniture for me."

Mutzi pounded the table with a fist, making all the glasses shake. "She bought more stuff for the lodge and lied about it."

Rose Ellen's face flush bright red. "I wanted the place to look nice." Her eyes shifted to Marge. "Nicer…more inviting for special guests who might influence more people to come to the lodge."

Chuck glanced around the table, watching people's reactions. Marge wrung her hands and pressed her lips tight. Roberto, who sat next to his wife, rolled his eyes and shook his head. Mutzi continued to fume.

The pieces of the puzzle started to fit together. The details led the authorities to him. "So, the can of money in the shed was for whatever Buddy sold for Rose Ellen?"

Sam nodded. "That's what he told authorities. He drove your truck, he wore your boots, and he stashed a thousand dollars in a can in the shed planning to give it to Rose Ellen in exchange for her silence."

Chuck rubbed his chin. "Silence about him being at the lodge." He turned to April and asked, "Is that why they let me go? Because Buddy confessed. Is he in detention?"

"Yes and no. It was his confession that got you released. But Buddy was smart enough to make a deal in exchange for information. He told them who bought the lamps and tables and where the officials could find him, provided they agreed to drop all charges. The guy was someone Buddy's father had previously done shady business with. The guy had a rap sheet for stealing and they found the rest of the money when they went to check out Buddy's story."

Sam drew in a deep breath and continued. "Some guy named Jasper took a picture of Chuck's truck at the mine. When he heard about the theft, he turned it into Corporal Duke in hopes of collecting a reward."

Chuck's eyes widened, and he stared at Sandi, remembering the guy at the restaurant. Surely, it wasn't the same man, but how many Jaspers lived in Dahlonega?

Sam continued. "Thankfully, children's services agreed to let Buddy stay with Father Mitch until they decided what needs to be done with him."

Mutzi added, "Pastor Mitch owed me one."

Sam shook his head. "There was some sad news. When the authorities tried to contact Buddy's father, they learned he died last month in a bar fight."

A collective gasp filled the room.

"It is sad, but I think Buddy was actually relieved. He feared his father. He said he thought his mother did too. She hasn't been seen or heard from since she took off two years ago. Buddy turns seventeen in a few weeks and won't need to be under children's services purview after that, provided he can support himself."

Chuck closed his eyes and said a silent prayer for the way things were turning out for Buddy. The tight pressure on his chest lessened. "Be sure they know he'll have a place to live and a job at the lodge, if he wants it."

The lodge. A shiver snuck up Chuck's back. In less than twelve hours, guests would be arriving. All the chores ignored while he was in jail waited for his attention. He pushed his chair back and stood in a panic. "There are a dozen things I still need to do. Chop more wood, finish trimming, order dog food—"

Marge touched his arm. "It's okay, Chuck. Sit down and finish your meal." She placed her other hand on Leroy's and smiled. "Leroy has taken care of everything. I think you'll find he's done a good job."

Chuck watched as the two shared an intimate moment. It filled his heart with joy to see Marge welcome another man into her life.

"Now it's my turn." Marge swept the table with her hand. "Everyone has stepped up and helped. Thank you. I don't know what we would have done without you." She drew her brows tight. "Who set the table for this meal?"

Mutzi grinned. "I did, and I sent out texts to everyone to bring food. Aren't you glad I used paper plates and plastic ware?"

"Yes. That was very thoughtful of you. Thanks, Sis." Marge turned and tipped her head toward Sandi. "I understand you brought two fully cooked turkeys. Where in the world did you find them at this late hour?"

"You were upset when I talked with you, so I pleaded with the Dahlonega Woman's Club for help. They let me come by the Community Center and pick up whatever you needed since they had more than enough to feed those who would come to the hall tomorrow."

"That was so sweet of you...and the women. I really should have been more help to them, but with the lodge opening, I didn't have the time." She shook her head and sighed.

"Speaking of time," Sandi said. "I hate to eat and run, but I need to get back to Atlanta."

"I wish you could stay, but I understand." Sandi gave Marge a hug.

Chuck stood and walked Sandi out.

"Thank you...again. I could hear your voice encouraging me whenever my faith faltered. You have no idea how special you are to me." It had only been a few days, but Chuck had missed her more than ever. He got lost in the black coffee pools that stared back at him.

"We'll talk soon. I promise. Have fun tomorrow. It's the beginning of a new journey and I think it's going to be a terrific adventure." She kissed his cheek and left.

The warm touch of her lips lingered as he watched her leave. He wasn't sure how long he stood there yearning for more. Suddenly famished, he returned to the dining hall and scarfed down the rest of his food.

When he finished, Marge cleared her throat. "Perhaps we should clean up before it gets too late."

Leroy stood. "Ladies, please stay seated. The men will take care of the table." He looked at Sam, Roberto, Paul, and Chuck with raised brows. "How about it, guys?"

From the looks on their faces, the others appeared to be caught as off-guard as Chuck, but they all stood and hurried to clear the food from the table.

Once in the kitchen, Chuck held the platter with the leftover chicken, staring in the pantry for something to put it in.

"Try this." Leroy offered a large plastic container. "Marge likes to use these because they're clear and she can see what's in them without taking the lid off."

It was evident Leroy had become quite familiar with Marge's routine. The guy seemed worthy of Chuck's endorsement despite their awkward first encounter. He extended a hand to Leroy. "I sincerely appreciate all you've done for my sister." With a wink, he added, "You do realize you are now part of the family. "

Leroy accepted the handshake. "I can think of worse things." A hint of a smile raised his cheek. "Your sister is pretty special."

Chuck agreed. "Yes. She is."

Leroy turned and walked out.

Chuck finished filling the dishwasher, pressed the start button, and headed back into the dining hall to see what else needed prepping for tomorrow. The room was empty, but he noticed a fresh set of place mats and napkins donned the table. He followed the chatter coming from the great hall. A sense of calm eased his shoulders. They really did have this under control.

Paul grinned as he cradled Savannah and walked toward Chuck. The innocent child slept soundly in his arms. "We need to head home. This one is past her bedtime."

April swept the room with her eyes as she stuffed the last abandoned teddy bear into the backpack slung over her arm. "Don't be offended, but I don't want to see you before Christmas." She smiled.

Chuck knew exactly what she meant. Stay out of jail. "Yes, ma'am. Thanks..." He tried to say more, but emotions obstructed his vocal cords. How could he possibly put into words the gratefulness stirring in his soul?

Across the room, Chuck watched Leroy whisper something to Marge, then kiss her cheek. He clenched his hat in one hand and waved as he walked past Chuck, into the kitchen, and out the back door. Their back-door friend. That's what Marge had called him. She'd explained it so simply. "He sees the mess, smells the mess, but he won't leave until he's helped cleaned up the mess." As far as Chuck could tell, Leroy represented the description quite well.

Before long, Roberto excused himself to return to Atlanta. Rose Ellen decided she'd stay over and be part of the lodge opening along with her siblings. Sam also left, leaving Chuck and his three sisters alone for the first time in days. They settled in front of the fireplace in silence.

All of them watched the flames dance and listened to the crackle of wood as it turned to ashes.

Mutzi stood and motioned for the others to do the same. "It's time."

Rose released a loud yawn. "Time for bed. I'm exhausted."

Marge stretched her back. "Did we forget to do something?"

"Just the most important part of this whole adventure." Mutzi opened the hall closet door and took out coats.

Chapter
Thirty-Three

A blanket of stars stretched to infinity across the near black sky. The crescent moon dangled miles above the slow drifting river which lapped the banks in barely a whisper. An earthy blend of water, soil, and pine swathed the dampness of the evening.

Each sibling searched the graveled path in silence for the perfect stone. Four wool blankets covered freshly cut tree stumps which formed a circle around the fire Leroy had built before he left. Once satisfied with their selection, they each claimed a seat.

Chuck's heart swelled as he glanced from one sister to the other. "Now what do we do?"

Rose Ellen held up a hand and cleared her throat. "No talking...yet. We spend a few minutes in silence identifying the differences between ballast and baggage in our lives. When we're ready, one person at a time speaks. No comments or interruptions." She placed a hand on her chest. "I'm the oldest, so I usually go first."

Mutzi grunted.

Following the instructions, Chuck stared off into the dark abyss. What things weighed him down? Anger, fear, regret. He couldn't change the events that created those emotions. The only thing he had control over was his reactions. His mind darted down alleys and roads that brought him to where he was today. He tried to imagine a fresh pathway. When he opened his eyes, his sisters smiled, each apparently ready for the next part of the process.

Rose Ellen turned to Marge. "This was your dream with George. I think you should go first."

The gracious suggestion seemed to surprise Marge. "Alright. Thank you." She adjusted her position on the stump. "I'm going to sit while I talk, if you don't mind."

A collective nod offered an opening for her to begin.

"For too long, I've filled every hour of every day volunteering, cooking, cleaning, sewing. I like helping others and having purpose. But I've realized what I really have been doing is avoiding being alone." She drew in a breath. "It's hard. And I'm tired. I didn't realize how tired until the day I fainted. I've always believed if you want it done right, do it yourself. Well, you've all taught me it can be done right even if it's not done the way I would do it.

"I'm getting too old to control things. So…I am resigning my position as president of the woman's club." She glanced toward Mutzi. "I'll still be a member, but it's time for someone younger to take over."

After a short pause, Marge added, "And, I'm going to rent out my house to college students. It's too big for me and too much work to keep it clean. I'll be living here full time." She pressed her lips and swallowed. "One last thing. I like Leroy and we're going to start dating. George says he likes him, too."

Even in the moonlight, Chuck could see the blush coloring her face. It tickled him to know her late husband gave her his blessings. "You've got my vote. He's a pretty good guy."

Rose Ellen chastised him for speaking. "My turn." She pulled her sweater jacket tight around her shoulders. "The last few weeks have opened my eyes to my…less than attractive behavior." She looked around the circle. "Go ahead, laugh. I didn't realize how bad I've gotten until we had that blow up at the lodge over the furniture. I was so worried you'd all hate me and never let me be part of this that I lied and worse than that, I got Buddy in so much trouble. I am sorry.

"Ever since my divorce—yes, it was decades ago—I decided I would never let anyone stomp on my heart again.

I became selfish and drew attention to myself however I could. Don't get me wrong, I liked having people wait on me and buying me expensive things, like Roberto used to do. But I didn't like myself. And no matter how much money I spent, the emptiness didn't go away. Someone once said 'Happiness resides not in possessions, and not in gold, happiness dwells in the soul.'

"My soul was empty. I'd pushed away everyone that I loved." She met each of their eyes. "I'm sorry. I know I can't change overnight. It's going to take some time to break old habits. But I'm really going to try. I want Savannah to grow up and be proud of her Nonna. Maybe I can teach her the difference between words like self-esteem and egotism, aggression and assertiveness. But I won't be doing it as her caregiver. She deserves better. I don't have the patience or energy to deal with that bundle of dynamite every day.

"I really want to be more involved with the lodge. I've been thinking about how I could help. If I come the last night of each session, I could help with the skipping stone gathering. Then, the next morning, I'd help change the linens, make the beds, and tidy the rooms. If that would be okay with you." She paused and then added, "I'm done. You can talk now."

Marge's eyes lit up and she glanced at Mutzi. "That would be wonderful. Don't you agree?"

Mutzi wrinkled her nose. "Wish I had a tape recorder. You better mean it because I'm going to hold you to it." Then she smiled. "Savannah's lucky to have you for a Nonna."

The tender comment touched Chuck's heart. As much trouble as the sisters gave each other, the love always surfaced stronger, more resilient than any other emotion.

Mutzi announced, "I'm going next. Our bro needs a little more time to prepare his words of wisdom."

He couldn't help but laugh at her boldness. It warmed his heart when she called him bro. She had a way of making it a cherished title. "You're right. I could use more time if you're expecting profound insightfulness from me."

Mutzi quieted and stared off toward the river's edge. "The journey with Sam took its toll on me this year. The long hours. The lack of his presence. I missed the attention he always showed me. There were days when I transgressed. I fell back into old habits. Superstitions inched their way back into my world and I spent too much time feeding them on the internet. Not only did I give Sam a tough time, Father Mitch paid the price, too."

The confession surprised Chuck. He hadn't realized the effect Sam's absence had on Mutzi. He'd been consumed with his own problems and had ignored what his sister was going through.

"I was scared. There's already a deacon at our church, so Sam would be sent to another parish outside of Dahlonega. As his wife, I'd be expected to follow him wherever he was assigned." She tucked a strand of hair behind her ear and paused. "I didn't make it easy for Sam to fulfill his calling. I wanted him to choose me. And even worse, I resented the fact that Sam loved God more than me." She choked on the words. "It hurt. It really hurt."

A tear trickled down her cheek. She swept it away.

"Father Mitch says he understands. I hope God does, too."

The ebony horizon lit for a brief second as a shooting star flashed across it.

Mutzi turned to the others. "Did you see that?" Her eyes wide with excitement. "I think that was God saying he gets it, too." She turned back toward the river and continued, "God was listening to my prayers. Maybe He knew I couldn't handle the changes." She raised her head high, looking toward the sky, and folded her hands as if in prayer. "Sam told me tonight that he is not going to become a deacon. Instead, he decided to offer counseling services through our church. Since he went through all the training, the dioceses approved his request. I'm going to support him without complaining. Maybe I'll even learn to cook." She turned toward her siblings. "That's enough emotions from me for one night. You're up, Chuck."

A thousand thoughts stirred in his mind. Putting them into words wouldn't be easy, but he respected the process his sisters followed to release and recover. It was time for him to do the same.

"Being locked away, alone, gives a mind lots of time to think. I found it hard to be grateful for anything while I was in there. Anger and resentment accumulated like thunder clouds before a storm. I was bitter and refused to cooperate with anything the sheriff wanted. I bitched about the food, the cell, music he played, and even cursed at the reporter who came each day trying to get me to tell her my story. The injustice of again being accused of a crime I didn't commit burned like a knife stabbed in the middle of my back with no way to reach it.

"Even when the sheriff released me, I lashed out at him. It wasn't his fault. He was doing his job, and he certainly went above and beyond his duties to make my stay as pleasant as could be. All I could think of was to retaliate by suing him and everyone involved. April tried to help me calm down. Instead of thanking her for picking me up, I ranted like an idiot on the drive to the lodge."

Chuck drew in a deep breath. "Anger doesn't fix any-thing. For every minute you are angry, you've given up a minute of peace. I want peace. When I toss that stone into the river, my wrath is going with it. I'm starting fresh, counting my blessings, and building a new reputation. Dragging the improper arrest out in court will do nothing but make the lawyers richer and me and Dahlonega poor-er.

"Instead, I'm going to contact that reporter and accept her offer to do a feature story. Maybe once folks read all the facts and circumstances, they'll see me differently. I'm not going to purposely make officials look bad, but hopefully, it will make them think twice before arresting the next innocent person.

"I've got apologies to make to April, the reporter, and the sheriff. Hopefully, Buddy comes back soon and I can help him work through the pains and frustrations he's had in his life. He needs to know what peace feels like and that there are more good people in this world than bad. We'll get him his own car. Maybe we can restore one together.

"You gals have believed in me and it's time I believed in myself. I've struggled with self-esteem for years and I'm tired of it. I'm a decent guy, worthy of a decent life. It's time I started believing in myself." He thought about Sandi's constant encouragement. Perhaps she was waiting for him to see what she sees. Maybe that's what was keeping her at arm's length. He didn't know, but he was going to get up enough courage to ask.

A chilling breeze stirred him back to the present. He stood and drew in a deep breath and released, slow and easy. "Are we ready?"

"Let's do it. I'm exhausted and ready for bed." Rose Ellen led the way.

With Chuck on one side and Mutzi on the other, they helped Marge to the river's edge. One by one, the stones splashed across the now choppy water and disappeared, taking the baggage that weighed each of them down. Thanksgiving Day was just a few hours away. What an appropriate way to begin the adventures of the Skipping Stone Lodge.

The End

Acknowledgements

It's been said it takes a village to raise a child. For me, it takes a community to write a novel. The members of Coffee and Critique, Sarah Angleton, Jeanne Felfe, Jane Hamilton, Alice Muschany, Doug Osgood, Les Thompson, Donna Volkenannt, Pat Wahler, and John (Jack) Zerr, have been my communal support group for a number of years and deserve a serious round of applause.

Their comments and suggestions added clever wit, improved my vocabulary choices, brought attention to grammar and punctuation errors, invited me to dig deeper into character development, pointed out plot missteps, and provided an endless amount of encouragement. Their imprints are visible in every chapter, nearly every page.

Saturday Writers, a non-profit organization of writers devoted to encouraging writers, and a chapter of the Missouri Writers Guild, is the cornerstone of my writing career. This remarkable group of more than one hundred writers has provided me with a network of experienced authors and a wealth of resources through their workshops, monthly guest speakers, and creative contest opportunities. Every community should have one.

Last but never least, to all of my family and friends who tolerate my endless tales about *The Dahlonega Sisters*. Whether you read versions of my manuscript, stood silently by my side while I pounded away on a keyboard, or offered encouragement in the slightest way, know that your support is appreciated. I love all of you.

About the Author

Born and raised in Missouri, Diane M. How is all about family and fun. When not reading, writing, or walking with her husband of 53 years, she enjoys basket weaving with her daughter, Laura.

Author of *The Dahlonega Sisters*, a women's fiction series, and *Burning Embers, Spark to Flame*, a romantic suspense, Diane is a member of the Missouri Writers Guild, St. Louis Writers Guild, and the treasurer of Saturday Writers, a non-profit organization of writers encouraging writers. More than thirty of her award-winning short stories and poems have been published in anthologies.

Normally not a world traveler, Diane embarked on her first trip outside the United States when she took an Eastern Caribbean cruise with Laura in 2023. Enchanted by the bold experience, she spread her wings wider in 2024 by flying to Rome and cruising the Mediterranean. Maybe she'll invite The Dahlonega Sisters along on her next voyage.